DEEP SOUTH DOCS!

Swapping the Big City...for the Bayou!

When two delectable doctors arrive in America's Deep South, looking for a fresh start, they soon find themselves falling for the charm of Bayou life—as well as for the attractions of the beautiful women they're working with!

But big-city surgeons with their bright ideas aren't always welcome in the Bayou. Especially when they're super-hot, heart-stopping distractions for the dedicated Deep South nurses. These women have enough complications as it is, without falling for the new docs in town…!

The second story
in Dianne Drake's *Deep South Docs* duet
A DOCTOR'S CONFESSION
is also available this month from
Mills & Boon® Medical Romance™

Dear Reader

When I went to Louisiana for the first time a few years ago—specifically New Orleans, and all the deep, dark backwoods of the bayou surrounding it—I knew I wanted to set a book there. It's a beautiful place, and there's nothing else quite like it in the United States. In fact, descriptions don't do it justice…but I've tried in this duet titled *Deep South Docs*.

Both stories, A HOME FOR THE HOT-SHOT DOC and THE DOCTOR'S CONFESSION, centre around the Doucet family and their daughters, all of whom work in the medical field in some capacity. In this duet you'll meet Mellette, who has to overcome one of life's greatest tragedies in order to find true love again. And you'll also meet Magnolia, who just can't seem to find time for love in her life.

Both meet men who try to capture their hearts, but it's not an easy thing to do as the Doucet family is filled with eight mighty strong women and one man who sits at the head of it and who's the biggest softie in the world. But, as both Justin Bergeron and Alain Lalonde discover, the fight is worth the effort…most of the time. At other times Mellette and Maggie are almost too much to handle.

When I was taking a boat ride through the swamps in the Louisiana bayou, perhaps the thing that fascinated me most were these little communities of people who live out there in the swamp, almost totally cut off from society. I could see the shacks almost everywhere. In fact we even took a detour by our tour guide's shack and saw a whole lot of alligators lounging in his front yard. He said that as long as he didn't bother them, they didn't bother him. Well, I don't know about that, but it certainly made for an interesting trip. So did the alligators that would swim right up to the boat.

I hope you enjoy your trip to the Louisiana bayous. It's fascinating. And after *this* trip to the bayous I'm going to hang around to write a few more books based in that part of the world, so look for Sabine and Delphine's stories coming next.

I like to hear from my readers, so please feel free to contact me at diannedrake@earthlink.net, or visit my website page at www.dianne-drake.com, from which you can link to either my Facebook page or my Twitter page.

As always, wishing you health & happiness

DD

A HOME FOR THE HOT-SHOT DOC

BY

DIANNE DRAKE

First published in Great Britain 2014
by Mills & Boon, an imprint of Harlequin (UK) Limited,
Large Print edition 2015
Eton House, 18-24 Paradise Road,
Richmond, Surrey, TW9 1SR

ISBN: 978-0-263-25452-5

Harlequin (UK) Limited's policy is to use papers that are natural, renewable and recyclable products and made from wood grown in sustainable forests. The logging and manufacturing processes conform to the legal environmental regulations of the country of origin.

Printed and bound in Great Britain
by CPI Antony Rowe, Chippenham, Wiltshire

Now that her children have left home, **Dianne Drake** is finally finding the time to do some of the things she adores—gardening, cooking, reading, shopping for antiques. Her absolute passion in life, however, is adopting abandoned and abused animals. Right now Dianne and her husband Joel have a little menagerie of three dogs and two cats, but that's always subject to change. A former symphony orchestra member, Dianne now attends the symphony as a spectator several times a month and, when time permits, takes in an occasional football, basketball or hockey game.

Recent titles by Dianne Drake:

A CHILD TO HEAL THEIR HEARTS
P.S. YOU'RE A DADDY
REVEALING THE REAL DR ROBINSON
THE DOCTOR'S LOST-AND-FOUND HEART
NO. 1 DAD IN TEXAS
THE RUNAWAY NURSE
FIREFIGHTER WITH A FROZEN HEART
THE DOCTOR'S REASON TO STAY**
FROM BROODING BOSS TO ADORING DAD
THE BABY WHO STOLE THE DOCTOR'S HEART*

***New York Hospital Heartthrobs*
**Mountain Village Hospital*

Praise for
Dianne Drake:

'A very emotional, heart-tugging story. A beautifully written book. This story brought tears to my eyes in several parts.'
—*GoodReads* Community Review on
P.S. YOU'RE A DADDY!

'An excellent story written with emotional depth and understanding.'
—*millsandboon.co.uk* Community Review on
FIREFIGHTER WITH A FROZEN HEART

CHAPTER ONE

NIGHTS LIKE THIS made him glad he was home again, if only for a little while. The far-off sound of bullfrogs bloating up and erupting with a courtly call to a lady love; the peculiar rhythm of the barred owl, who called to his own love from high atop the cypress trees; the warm breeze blowing in over the water and carrying with it the unique, earthy scent of the swamp… This all meant home to Dr. Justin Aloysius Bergeron. Home, but with that came so many mixed, even conflicting feelings.

With a mug full of sassafras tea and its bitter, soothing flavor, and a plate of his own home-made beignets made from his grandmother's recipe, Justin was ready to settle in on the porch swing for the evening and simply relax after a long day of doing nothing. Absolutely nothing. Nothing took a lot of effort for someone who was used to being active, all that sitting around and thinking. Down here, where life was slower, it wore him out more than a day on his feet in the O.R. did. Those were physically exhausting days, but here his exhaustion was emotional and far heavier. It dragged him down to a place where a good night's sleep didn't bring about any kind of recovery.

At a month shy of thirty-six, Justin was at the top of his game back in Chicago. He was well respected as a general surgeon with a career pointed in the direction of chief of services, or so he hoped. Equally well respected as a medical mystery writer with a couple of prestigious awards under his belt and talk of a movie in the works. It took a lot of effort, cranking out all that career, which was why all this nothingness seemed so strange to him.

He wasn't used to it, wasn't used to being lazy. But lazy was exactly what he was being, and it was turning him dull and lethargic, which, for the moment, suited him just fine. Because until he figured out his next move, nothing was truly all he wanted to concentrate on. He wrote in the early, early morning, as was his habit, but then there was nothing to occupy his time or to occupy his mind for the rest of the day. He was trying not to think outside the pages he'd managed to bang out. He was succeeding, intermittently.

For sure, life was simpler here in the Louisiana bayou than it was back in Chicago, his home for the past decade. He hadn't appreciated that singular simple fact when he'd lived here before. In fact, from the time he had been a teenager, all he'd ever wanted had been to get away from the simplicity. Go to the city. Any city. Seek out excitement and anything else that didn't resemble the upbringing he was accustomed to—an upbringing with a down-home flavor that could only be found in the bayou. Or the backcountry. Or godforsaken nowhere. Or, as this area had been named by its early settlers, Big Swamp.

And he'd done all that. Molded himself into what he'd wanted to be, and set off to become it. Self-made man, he'd called himself in the early days, even though now he knew better. Nobody with the kind of love and support he'd had was self-made, and just thinking about how he used to brag about his self-sufficiency caused him to cringe now. Even so, he was successful. Wealthy. Some considered him a player, although he wasn't sure he liked that description since he really didn't have time to play. But it bolstered the image. Playboy. Sports car. Condo on the lakeshore. Medical practice in the high-end Magnificent Mile. Everything about him shooting to the top.

But Justin was also part of Big Swamp—something he was just now beginning to admit. Big Swamp, where his grandmother had done her level best to raise a wayward young boy who hadn't wanted to be raised, hadn't wanted to follow the rules, hadn't wanted anything to do with an old-fashioned set of values that had done his grandmother well for her eighty-nine years on earth. Yes, that was all him, too. The part of him he didn't talk about, or admit to. The part of him he wouldn't deny but certainly wouldn't confirm, either. It had been part of his embarrassment back then, part of his pride now.

No, none of this had been good enough for the young Justin. In a way it wasn't even enough for the Justin who existed now; he certainly hadn't made himself right with it. Hence the emotional exhaustion. But at least Justin felt more remorse for his attitude than he'd expected he ever would. And now that Grandma Eula was gone, his regrets weighed him down. Especially on an unsullied night like this, the kind of night she would have loved, where Big Swamp was at peace with itself. And yet Justin was not.

He missed Bonne-Maman Eula, as she'd been called by the people who loved her. More than that, he lamented…so much. And his grief felt so heavy against his heart, at times almost stopping it from beating. He'd owed her better, had always thought there was more time to do better for her. He'd always intended to.

"Now it's too late," he said to Napoleon, his grandmother's big, lazy, orange-striped tomcat. A fourth-, maybe fifth-generation Napoleon, actually. There'd always been a big, orange-striped tomcat living here for as long as Justin could remember, and his name had always been Napoleon. This Napoleon seemed especially mellow, he thought. More mellow than the earlier ones, and it made Justin wonder what the cat knew that he did not.

"I've been thinking lately that she'd want you to stay on here," Amos Picou said as he stepped up onto the wooden porch and took his customary seat on the well-worn wicker chair next to Justin's porch swing. The same chair he'd been sitting in for every one of the twenty-five years he'd come visiting.

It had been Eula's favorite chair—her chair of honor, she'd called it, because of its high, fan-shaped back. She'd loved that chair as it had reminded her of a throne, and she had spent many of her evenings sitting in it. Said it made her feel like royalty because she sat so high and mighty, which was why she'd always offered to let her guests sit in it, because in her house guests had always been treated like royalty.

In a way, Eula Bergeron had been royalty in that part of Big Swamp. There'd been no one more trusted or respected. With the way she'd been held in such high esteem in her community, there was no other way to describe it. Justin's grandmother had been treasured, and that was something he hadn't seen so much back in his childhood as he'd been too busy seeing other things—dreams, or delusions, of a better life mostly. Life away from here, somewhere, anywhere other than Big Swamp. Something other than what his grandmother had given him.

He hadn't appreciated her enough, and that had played on his mind more than he probably even recognized. Those sleepless nights, guilt trips, wanting to make it up to her when he could, feeling like hell after it was too late.

Now that he was back for a little while to tie up loose ends, he was reminded of all the respect for his grandmother everywhere he looked. "Not sure what I'm going to do, Amos," Justin said, his voice betraying his lackluster mood. "Can't stay here, but I don't want to walk away from the people who depended on my grandmother and leave them with nothing."

"Folks in these parts need them a good doctor now that your Bonne-Maman Eula has left us. They'd be mighty grateful if you stayed on to look after them. I think Eula would have approved of that, getting you back home where you belong."

"Except I don't belong here now." Justin exhaled an exasperated breath. "Too many years, too much separation… Besides, she knew how I felt about coming home for good. Knew I didn't want any part of it, that short visits to see her were the best I could do."

"She knew that, boy. Knew you loved what you were doing, where you were doing it. All she wanted was for you to be happy."

"And I was…am. But…" He shrugged his shoulders. "I don't know how to explain it.

"Torn between your worlds."

"Did she ever tell you I asked her to come live with me in Chicago?"

"She had a good laugh over that. Appreciated

the gesture, laughed at the idea of living in such a city. I lived there for a while once upon a time. Can't say that I hated it, but it sure didn't fit me. And it sure wouldn't have fit Eula, either."

"I wanted to buy her a condo in New Orleans."

"Which kept her closer to home, which would have probably been even worse for her, so close and yet so far away from it." He shook his head. "Eula was a single-minded woman and it was a mind you weren't going to change. Not for any reason outside of you needing someone to take care of you."

"Maybe I should have lied."

"Or left it the way she wanted."

"The way she wanted it..." He pulled a crumpled letter from his pocket. "'You'd be a good doctor here, Justin. Promise me you'll think about it.' Well, I've been thinking. That's all I've been doing and I don't understand how she could have asked that of me. She knew better."

"I supposed she did, but do you?"

"I can't stay here and dispense herbs. That's all there is to it."

"Dispense herbs, get the folks in the area used to traditional medicine. Sounds to me that's exactly what she wanted from you."

"But I can't do it! She'd asked me before, I'd told her no. Then she'd told me I'd know when it was time to come home. But I can't just come home. Home is Chicago now. In a penthouse overlooking the lakeshore, senior member of a general surgery practice. That's home."

"You're sounding awfully defensive about it, boy."

"Because I am defensive about it. I've worked hard at setting up the life I want, and I'm not about to change that to come back here."

"Ah, but you could compromise, couldn't you? You, know...practice what you want most of the time, slip in a little bit of what they want every now and again? Make everybody happy."

Yes, right. Make everybody happy but him. "You are persistent, old man. Gotta give you credit for that." In spite of the man's almost daily nagging, Justin liked him. Always had. Amos Picou was ageless, with his unflawed black skin that showed no wrinkles, no age. Like Napoleon, Amos had come around for as long as Justin could remember, bringing his grandmother gator steaks, crawfish and whatever other food he managed to scrounge in Big Swamp. He'd always gone herb hunting with Eula, too, claiming Big Swamp was no place for a woman alone. Unrequited love, Justin suspected. Although he'd never asked and Amos had never told.

Rumor had it, though, that Amos had a little herb patch of his own, something he grew, cured and smoked. Perhaps that was the secret to his longevity and youth.

"That's the only way you get what you want, son. If you want it bad enough, you go after it and don't give up till it's dead, or till you're dead. That's what my granddaddy always taught me." He grinned. "Compromise is good for the soul, too. It'll make you feel like you're in a giving spirit, yet you have the good feeling that comes along with a victory of getting what you want. Best of both worlds, I always say."

"But when you say you want me to compromise, you mean give up everything I've worked hard to get, just so I can come here and dispense swamp morning glory to cure centipede bites to a bunch of people who hate me? Because that's not me, Amos." He shook his head vigorously. "I have a great respect for my grandmother's herbal cures, but for me life here is tough. Too tough. I don't fit in and I never have. That's what I ran away from when I was a kid, and I'm sure as hell not planning on coming back to it. That's why I hired that nurse to come in and help my grandmother—to keep me away from the medicine here. So maybe she's the one you should be trying to convince to take over, since all I've heard for the past year is glowing reports."

His grandmother had called Mellette Chaisson a godsend. He'd called her the compromise he'd needed to assuage his guilty feeling at not being the one to help his grandmother. The worst of it was, a traveling nurse who spent two days a week here assuaged a lot of his guilt. Just not all of it.

"That nurse was a real blessing for your grandmother, especially getting on toward the end. But she's not the solution here now, and you know that."

Yes, he did know that, which was why he was passing his days and nights only writing. Writing was where he could escape, a different world. A place with no guilt. "What I know is that I'm doing the best I can for the people here. I support that nurse coming in, and I'll continue to do that. Even up her presence here if that's what needs to happen."

"But what about the other days of the week, Justin? If we get sick, if somebody gets hurt, do we just wait until she comes back? Put our aches and pains on hold until her next day on duty?"

"You take a twenty-five-mile trip to the nearest hospital. This area of the bayou may be remote, but it's not entirely cut off from civilization."

Amos laughed out loud over that. "Whose universe are you living in, boy? Because you know the people here aren't makin' that trip. They keep to themselves, don't step foot in the big city unless it's absolutely necessary, go over to Grandmaison only when it's necessary, and they never,

ever, look for medical help outside Big Swamp. That's just the way things are around here."

"Then that's their problem, because help's available."

"And it was your grandmother's problem, because she doctored these people every day of her life."

"She gave them herbs, Amos. The rest of it was…" He wanted to say hysteria, or emotional dependence, but that would be downplaying what his grandmother had done for the isolated people in Big Swamp, and he sure didn't want to do that. "I'm not my grandmother. I don't have her knowledge of herbs. Can't be what anybody here wants."

"Can't, or won't?"

"Same difference. Anyway…" He shrugged. "Let me think on it some more, try to figure out what's best."

"You know what's best, boy. Seems to me you're spending all your time trying to figure your way around it. And it's not like we expect you to be here all the time. Keep that nurse coming in two days, then use some of that city money you make and fly down here for two days yourself. Or maybe transfer your fine medical skills to one of the hospital establishments in New Orleans to make it easier on you. That would work. Would suit us just fine, too."

Amos pulled out one of his homemade cigarettes, tamped down the end of it, then stuck it in his mouth and lit it up. "But here you sit, all bound up with some heavy confusion," he said, letting the first long draw settle into his lungs.

"Here I sit because I'm tying up my grandmother's affairs," Justin said defensively.

A deep, rumbling laugh started from what seemed like the pit of Amos's belly and burbled its way out. "Tying up her affairs, my ass," he said, offering Justin a hit of his cigarette.

Justin refused.

"You're here because you got yourself caught someplace between heaven and hell, and you don't know which way to turn. Part of you is pulling to go one way but part of you is holding back for some reason you probably don't even understand yet." Amos took another draw of his cigarette, and chuckled. "You're confused, boy. Just plain confused."

"Not denying it," Justin said, taking another sip of tea. "I'm confused, and I feel guilty as hell that I didn't know she was sick. Guilty that I didn't come back to see her as much as I would have if I'd known. I mean, I loved my grandmother, but..."

"But you didn't make her life easy."

"Not when I was a boy." He'd tried harder when he was a man, though.

"And now that you're a man you're paying for something she'd long ago forgot. She didn't hold it against you, boy. In fact, she was proud of what you made of yourself. Bragged on it all the time."

"And didn't tell me she was sick."

"Because you would have stuck her in some fancy hospital where she didn't want to go."

"If she'd gone she might not have..." He bit his tongue to hold back the bitterness. It didn't matter. Choices had been made; he hadn't been included. "Anyway, I'm trying to figure it out. I'll be talking to the nurse, and I'll see if she can give you another day. But that's the best I can do."

"The best you can do is admit you're still one of us, and give us that day yourself. Would have been Eula's wish."

"Damn it, Amos! I can't just commute from Chicago one day a week, and I'm not going to transfer to a New Orleans hospital to be closer. Also, I'm not one of you, which is the biggest problem. I never was. Not even when I was a kid, and you know that."

"That's right, city boy. You come from spoiled uppity folks who never would step foot in Big Swamp for fear something might bite them, or dirty their pretty little leather shoes." He kicked his foot up, showing up a well-worn, holey sneaker that had seen better days a decade ago. "I do have me a fine pair of alligator boots I save for special occasions, but that's not good enough for the Bergerons who left these parts."

"Would that be me?" Justin asked, knowing in some ways it was. He'd been from the city, raised there until he was five, then dumped on a grandmother he'd never met when his parents had died in a plane crash.

"If you want it to be, boy. Only if you want it to be."

The problem was, while his formative years had been spent in Big Swamp, he'd turned uppity, as it was called in these parts. But only after walking a long, hard road to get there. "Never mine, *mon cher,*" his grandmother had said to him on many occasions. "You've still got the good in you." *The good.* Whatever that was.

After the way he'd behaved he wasn't sure the good she'd seen was still there. If it ever had been.

His grandmother had loved him dearly, though. Taken him in without question when asked, raised him the best way she'd known how. And loved him. Dear God, that woman had possessed such a capacity for love. Along with the same generous capacity for forgiveness and understanding.

"What I want…" Justin paused. Listened to the same barred owl he'd been listening to earlier, then sighed. "Don't have a clue." Not a clue, except that he couldn't stay here.

"Sure you do, boy. It's just going to take some strong medicine to cure you—something that's stronger than anything you can prescribe." Amos took another draw on his cigarette, then stood up. "Got me a couple dozen fresh eggs and a loaf of Miss Minnie's bread, made fresh this afternoon. Caught me a whole mess of crawfish today, too. So I'm fixing up a fine scramble for breakfast in the morning. Bring some peppers and onions and I'll see you around six."

"Nine," Justin countered. "And no chicory in the coffee."

"Seven-thirty, city boy. And it's not coffee if it doesn't have chicory. So don't be late, or I'll be startin' without you." He smacked his lips. "Havin' those crawfish all for myself."

Okay, so part of Big Swamp was in his blood. He loved crawfish and wasn't ashamed to admit it. He missed the way his grandmother had fixed them. "Fine, seven-thirty. But not a minute earlier. And go easy on the hot sauce, old man," Justin said as Amos ambled off the porch. "Don't want to burn my tongue off."

Amos's only reply was another one of his belly laughs.

Rather than dragging a reluctant child up the sidewalk, Mellette gave in and picked up the protesting three-year-old Leonie and carried her the length of the pavement. Passing by the red azaleas and pink bougainvillea, walking under a drape of lavender wisteria, which she'd dearly loved since she was a child, she struggled the squiggling bundle up the steps of the white plantation mansion, on past the massive columns supporting the front porch overhang, and straight to the mahogany doors. "I'll be home before you're in bed," she said as she fought to grab hold of the doorknob.

"Why can't I come with you?" Leonie whined.

"Because I don't have time to watch you." And there were alligators, and the swamp, and all manner of other outdoor things that weren't safe for a three-year-old who lived to escape her mother's watchful eye. "Mommy has patients to see all day." And Mommy was beginning to wear down from the daily grind of her work, which meant she wasn't as alert as she needed to be. Not alert enough, anyway, to take care of a day's worth of patients as well as look after a rambunctious toddler who, every day, in every way, was growing to be more and more like her daddy. Something that warmed Mellette's heart, and broke it at the same time.

"I told you we'd take care of those bills," Zenobia Doucet said sharply as she took Leonie from Mellette. "You're killing yourself, working so hard. And your daughter needs you. Just look at her—she's wild. And you... You're a mess. Doucet women should look better, Mellette. And if you weren't working out there in the bayou..."

Instinctively, she pushed her short hair back from her face. "But I am working in the bayou. And I'm hoping that job is still there for me now that Eula's gone." She worked there to help pay off medical bills left over from Landry's illness. They were her responsibility, and she took her responsibilities seriously. "One more year, and I'll be free and clear. Then I won't have to moonlight." One more year and she'd be so ready to move on.

"Darling, you lost your house, they took away your car...you and my granddaughter live in a one-room apartment. You need better than that, and your father and I—"

"And we're making it work, Mother," she interrupted, brushing a kiss on her mother's cheek.

"But you don't have to be so proud about it. We're family, and family's supposed to help."

Sometimes it was still hard to believe that Landry was gone, because everything in her life revolved around him. But he was, had been for over two years now. A short bout with a devastating cancer, and she'd been widowed with a baby. Left with insurmountable debt she wouldn't let her family take over for her. Landry had been a proud man and she'd loved that about him. She had her own pride, too. And sure, a bailout from her family would have been easy. Move in, take money. But it wasn't right. She and Landry had agreed on that before his death. Although now Mellette was sure Landry hadn't known the extent of debt left to her. But that was okay. It was their agreement, something she had to do to honor his memory. And, yes, she was prideful, because she wanted to be an example for her daughter. Wanted not only to teach her strength but show her strength.

So she worked two jobs, raised a daughter and made one concession on child care, not just because her family doing it for free was helpful—which it was. But if she couldn't spend much time with her daughter these days, she at least wanted her daughter in the arms of people who loved and cherished her. Mellette's father, a retired anesthesiologist, spent his days with Leonie. Her mother, an active physician and chief of staff at New Hope Medical Center, spent evenings with Leonie when that was necessary. Her six sisters—all medical in one capacity or another—took turns when they could. And it worked beautifully.

They were an eminently qualified family to

care for one little girl. And a family who loved Leonie with a passion. So Mellette had no qualms about leaving her daughter with them, except that she was missing out, and that hurt. Because her mother was correct. Leonie needed more of her. "I love you and Daddy for wanting to help me but, like I've told you, it's working out."

"But it breaks my heart, seeing how hard you're working. Seeing how it's dragging you down like it is."

"What I need most is to know that Leonie's in good hands. She's my biggest concern, and it makes me feel a lot better knowing you all have her when I can't."

"Your father and I would never refuse her, and you know that. And if you ever change your mind..."

"I know," Mellette said, glancing at her watch. One hour until her first patient arrived, and she still had to take that hellish boat ride in. Sure, she could drive in, but it took twice as long and that extra time the boat afforded her was time she spent with Leonie. "Look, I'm running behind. Got patients to see, and I'm barely going to beat them to the door. I'll be back tonight, but it's going to be a late day because I need to get some things straight with Justin. So go ahead and keep Leonie for the night, and I promised her I'd be back to tuck her in. Although I'm not sure she'll be awake when I get here. And if you don't mind, I'll probably crash here tonight, as well."

"Or you could just move home," Zenobia said again. "Lord knows, we have plenty of room."

Yes, they did have the room. But Mellette needed her private time with Leonie, and their tiny apartment suited them for now.

Mellette gave her mother another kiss on the cheek. "Tell Daddy I love him, and that maybe I'll see him later tonight." She gave her daughter a kiss. "And you, young lady, need to be good for your grandmother. Promise?"

Leonie gave her mother a sullen look and didn't answer. Which made Mellette's load even heavier to bear. But there was nothing she could do right now. One more year, though, and things would be different. Just one more year…

* * *

Mellette Chaisson. Justin really didn't know much about her. He'd hired her from the registry, had liked her credentials. Had liked her voice over the phone during the interviews. Liked what he'd seen of her bedside manner, as well. But when she was here he pretty much stayed away because the people trusted her with their problems. Whereas they were wary around him. So he didn't want to shake up that dynamic, which meant that the days she was here, he wasn't. From what he'd seen in passing, though, he did like her. Especially the way she threw herself into her work.

Except she always looked tired. "They're lining up today," he told her, as she rushed through the kitchen and quickly stowed a couple of bottles of water and a sandwich in the fridge.

"There's a flu virus going around. Ever since we had that malaria come though, people get nervous with the least little sniffle."

"People overreact."

She arched her back, bared her claws at that

insensitive remark. "Four people in the community died of malaria, Doctor. If that causes the rest of them to overreact, then I suppose they have a right to. And you know what? While you may pay my salary, you're really not entitled to an opinion since you don't get involved in anything other than putting a signature on a check."

Okay, so maybe liking her was too strong. He admired her dedication to her work. Didn't know a thing about her, though. Not a single thing. Except she wore a wedding ring. Had a fiery temper. And she was a good nurse. Of course, his grandmother had liked her, too, and that said a lot. "So what you're telling me is that your employer isn't allowed to express an opinion about his employee's work."

"Yes," she said, quite sternly. "And, technically, I was not your employee. I worked for your grandmother, who worked for the community."

He couldn't help but smile. "Then that makes me…what?"

"Right now, a nuisance. Go to work, see a few of those couple dozen people out there who want to be seen, and I could be persuaded to change my mind about that. Otherwise get out of my way."

Mellette slammed through the kitchen door, hurried down the hall and into the area Eula had set aside for her clinic. The people waiting there were orderly and polite, no one pushing and shoving to be seen first. But there were so many of them, she was beginning to wonder if she'd be able to make good on that promise to tuck her daughter in tonight, because if she wasn't out of here by dusk, she wasn't going.

Travelling during the daylight was one thing, and she'd gotten used to that. But Big Swamp at night was a whole different story, and not one she particularly wanted to face. Call her a coward, call her chicken…she'd answer to it all because she was a city girl. Hadn't even known these isolated pocket communities existed in Big Swamp until a year ago when she'd seen the ad for a part-time nurse. And she'd spent her entire life living so close to here.

Talk about an isolated existence! Raised with

all the advantages, she was almost embarrassed to admit where she'd lacked. Landry had made up for that in a lot of ways, not being from that proverbial silver-spoon family, like she was. But all this… Areas where an entire community of people existed, totally out of step with society, living a good life independently. Nothing was taken for granted here. And every kind gesture was appreciated.

"I don't work here," Justin said, following her into the clinic, which had actually been his grandmother's parlor. Now it was a plain room with several wooden chairs and a curtain to separate the waiting area from the person being seen. There was nothing medicinal here. No equipment, no real medicines. Of course, Eula Bergeron hadn't practiced medicine. She'd been a self-taught herbalist. Someone who'd known which swamp herbs cured what.

"But you could, since you're not doing anything else."

"The people don't trust me."

"Probably because you've given them good reason not to."

"You're actually right about that. So what's the point of wasting my time?"

"What's the point of even being here if you're not going to make yourself useful?" she snapped. "Look, we need to talk. Today. Later."

"You're right. I was thinking about asking you to put in another day every week."

"Another day?" Mellette sputtered. "And just where would I get that?"

Justin shrugged. "I assumed..."

She stepped around him, and gestured her first patient to the area behind the cabinet. "Don't assume anything about me, Doctor. And while you're at it, don't presume, either. Now, if you'll excuse me, I have patients who need medical care. If you're not willing to provide it, get out!"

She pointed to the front door without another word. But what was there to say? Justin Bergeron was an annoyance. If she hadn't heard Eula mention him so much this past year, she would have never guessed this man and the veritable *saint*

Eula had talked about so lovingly were one and the same. But they were, and she wondered about the discrepancy. Wondered a whole lot.

CHAPTER TWO

IT WAS HARD watching her work, and doing nothing himself. She had such a look of determination, though. Brown eyes narrowed to her task. Biting down in concentration on her lower lip. He did have to admit Mellette was a looker. Tall, with legs that went on forever. Nice athletic form with well-defined feminine muscles. Smooth, dark skin, boyish-cut black hair with just a hint of natural curl, and all of it thrown into her work while he stood on the sidelines, casually observing.

But that was the way his days went since people around here would hardly even speak to him outside a stiff hello or an unfriendly nod accompanied by a muffled grunt. So what the hell made him think they'd accept him as a doctor? Someone to trust, someone to confide in. Someone to take care of them the way his grandmother had.

Clovis Fonseca, for example. He was waiting in line to have Mellette see him—Justin wasn't sure why—and if it weren't for the fact that Justin had stolen his canoe some twenty-five years ago, then gone and torn a hole in the bottom of it by racking it up on a cypress stump, Clovis might have been inclined to let Justin take a look at him. But Clovis held a grudge, and Justin had seen it every time he'd looked in the man's eyes since he'd come home. There was no way Clovis would ever consent to a physical exam from Justin, probably just as Clovis would probably never even greet him with anything other than a snarly sort of a snort.

And Ambrosine Trahan. He felt really bad about her because she'd loved him when they'd been kids, but he'd blatantly asked out her younger sister, Emmy Lou, the prettier of the two girls. It hadn't been so much that he'd wanted to go out with Emmy Lou, because he hadn't. She hadn't been his type, either. But he'd simply been trying to rebuff Ambrosine because back in the day he hadn't gone out with girls who hadn't been pretty. In fact, he'd been known to be intentionally cruel to them. So she was waiting in line today, a beautiful woman now, by all estimations, probably hanging on to horrible memories of the way he'd treated her, and he seriously doubted she'd want to claim him as her doctor. And rightfully so. He was so embarrassed just remembering the way he'd treated her.

The problem was, the line of waiting patients was full of bad experiences left over from his ill-mannered youth, and he didn't trust any of them to trust him. And who could blame them? He'd been a repeat offender on all fronts. After he'd taken Clovis's boat, he'd had pretty much the same experience with Rex Rimbaut's pickup truck. Taken it, banged it up. Then there had been that time he'd flaunted a date with Ambrosine's cousin, Ida, in front of both Ambrosine and Emmy Lou. Ida had been pretty. He'd done the same with their other cousin, Marie Rosella, as well, who had been even prettier.

So nothing gave Justin reason to believe that any one of those people waiting to be seen by

Mellette would believe that he'd turned over that new leaf. Especially when each and every one of them assumed he'd neglected his grandmother at the end of her life. It was something that overshadowed everything else. And no one knew the real story, that she'd purposely not told him she was failing for fear that he'd want to do something drastic, like move her to the big city, rather than let her die where she wanted to.

No, history wouldn't repeat itself on his account. But as far as the people here were concerned, twenty-five years ago was the same as yesterday, and time wasn't healing the bad thoughts they had of him. He was Justin Bergeron, bad boy. Poor Eula's pitiful excuse for a grandson.

And poor Eula's pitiful grandson wasn't welcome to touch them, not for any reason. They'd just as soon go without medical help as accept his.

Which made Justin feel like hell, seeing how hard Mellette was working while all he was doing was standing around, twiddling his thumbs and wallowing in his just desserts.

"Anything I could do where they wouldn't see me?" he finally asked her, as she rushed into the kitchen to grab a drink of water. Looking frazzled. But sexy frazzled.

"Right. Like you really want to work," she said, not even trying to hide her contempt for him.

"I'm not saying I *want* to work. But I am saying I would, if I could." It was either that or go back to his writing, and today, like yesterday and the day before that, he wasn't in that frame of mind. In spite of an upcoming deadline, there were too many distractions. Too many things to think about. Too many humiliating memories floating around in his mind, pushing out the intelligible words that might have gone down on paper.

"Then just do it, Doctor. The only way these people are ever going to get over their grudges against you is to see you do something worthwhile. Otherwise, in their eyes, you're still a bad boy who gave his grandma more grief than she needed." She tossed him a devious smile. "And a bad doctor who lets me work my fingers to the bone while he's standing around, making an ass of himself, doing nothing to help. So take your pick…ass or bad boy."

"Do I get a third choice?"

"Two's the limit around here. So what's it going to be?" She took a swig out of the water bottle, then recapped it. "Because two people off my list and onto yours might make the difference between me making it home to tuck my daughter into bed tonight or being stuck here all night, since I don't negotiate Big Swamp alone after dark."

So she had a wedding ring *and* a daughter. Interesting information—not that he wanted to be involved with her in any way other than professionally. But he did enjoy these brief glimpses into her life and wondered what else he might see if he paid attention. "Okay, let me see what I can do." With that, Justin went to the waiting area, then continued on through and opened the front door so the people standing around on the porch and in the yard could hear his announcement.

"For what it's worth, I'm a fully qualified medical doctor. I'm sure my grandmother mentioned that to all of you at one point. I know there are a few…several of you who probably don't want me seeing you on a professional basis, and I do understand why. But if there are any of you who'd let me examine you, I'd be glad to do so. And the fewer people Mrs. Chaisson has to see, the sooner she'll get home to her…family. So I'll be in the kitchen. If you're not still holding a grudge against me, I'll be glad to see you. Actually, I'll be glad to see you even if you are still holding a grudge. Either way…" He shrugged, then stepped back inside and immediately looked at Mellette, who was standing near the room divider, smiling.

"Seriously?" she said. "That's how you tell people you're open for business? It sounded more like a challenge than an invitation. You know, come stand in my line, if you dare."

"Best I can do. If the folks here want to see me, now they know they can. And if they don't, I'll be in the kitchen, cooking up a pot of gumbo." Fixing gumbo, practicing medicine, all in the same room. What had he been thinking?

* * *

"But that's not what Eula had me taking," Miss Willie Bascomb scolded. "And you should know better than to give me the wrong thing, young man. Do you think I'm too old to see what you're trying to do to me, switching off my medicine the way you are? It's shameful. Just shameful!" She was a gray-haired lady with sharp eyes and an even sharper tongue.

"But it's a simple anti-inflammatory for your arthritis," Justin said. "The prescription's easily filled at any pharmacy, and I can write you a script for ninety days so you won't have to go to town for it very often." Her knuckles were enlarged, fingers slightly bent into an outward curve. Nothing about Miss Willie had changed since he'd been a kid, and her condition seemed stable for the most part, but he didn't want to prescribe an herbal potion when the market was full of great prescription drugs that could prevent further joint damage.

"But I don't want me no prescription, Justin Aloysius. What your grandma gave me has worked well for as long as I can remember. Cures the aches, and that's all I need." She held up her crippled hands. "They haven't gotten any worse in all this time, and it's just plain foolish, wanting me to change my medicine when things are going well. Eula wouldn't have allowed that." She wagged a scolding forefinger at him. "And shame on you for trying."

The only problem was Eula wasn't here, and he couldn't duplicate her herbal cures, which for Miss Willie's condition was sassafras combined with prickly ash, cayenne and camphor, made into what his grandmother had called her rheumatism liniment. So in practical terms he was wasting his time with this patient because she wasn't about to budge, just as he wasn't. "Then I think we have a problem, because I can't give you what my grandmother used to make. Even if I wanted to, which I don't, I don't know how to make it."

"Because you were off gallivanting in the big city when you should have been staying home, studying *real* medicine, young man!" Miss Willie sniffed indignantly. "I wanted to give you a chance for Eula's sake. She talked so highly of you, said you were the best doctor there is. But she was wrong, and it would have killed her to see just how sorry you are."

Talk about a bitter pill to swallow. "All I can do is recommend what my kind of medicine considers standard. It's up to you whether or not you want to take it."

"What I want to take is my leave, young man!" With that, Miss Willie slid off the kitchen stool, gathered up her patent-leather purse, which she stuffed into the crook of her arm, and her floral print scarf, which she didn't bother putting on her head, and headed for the kitchen door. "You tell Mellette I want my usual. She'll know how to fix it for me."

Then she was gone. Miss Willie and all her one hundred pounds of acrimonious fire stormed out the back door, but not before she'd looked in the pot of gumbo and snorted again. "I don't smell filé in there," she said. "To make a good gumbo you've got to use filé powder, or do you have some fancy prescription for that, too?"

"Seems like sassafras is going to be your downfall today," Mellette said, walking into the kitchen through the front door at the same time the back door slammed shut. She was referring to filé, a thickening powder made from dried sassafras leaves.

"She always was a tough old lady," Justin replied, on his way to the kitchen cabinet to look for filé. "Who wants what she wants."

"She swears by the liniment. Don't think she's going to change her mind about that, and at her age I guess that's her right."

"But I can't give her the damned liniment." He turned to look at her. "And as a registered nurse, I'm surprised you would."

"When you hired me to come to Big Swamp to help your grandmother, what did you expect me to do? Dispense pills these people don't want to take? That's not what Eula wanted, not what she would have tolerated from me. So she taught me her ways and for the most part it works out."

"So I'm paying you to practice my grandmother's version of medicine? Because that's not what I wanted."

"What you wanted was to have me help her, which was what I did. On her terms, though. Not yours."

"If I'd wanted someone to dispense more of what my grandmother dispensed, that's who I would have hired. But I wanted a registered nurse, someone from the traditional side of medicine. Someone to take care of the people here the way traditional medicine dictates."

"Then I expect you've been paying me under false pretenses because I've been taking care of these people just the way your grandmother did and, so far, nobody's complaining."

"You're still doing that even now that she's gone?"

"Especially now that she's gone. They're scared to death they're going to have to give up the folk medicine they've trusted for decades, and I suppose if you have your way, that's what's going to happen. Which just adds to the list of reasons why they don't like you."

He pulled a tin marked filé from the cabinet and measured out a scant spoonful for the gumbo.

"Twice that much," she prompted him.

"You're a chef, as well?"

"I know how your grandmother fixed gumbo, and I'm assuming you're trying to copy that since it's probably the best gumbo I've had anywhere."

He shook his head, not sure if he should be angry or frustrated. Or both. "So tell me, how am I supposed to treat Miss Willie when she won't take a traditional anti-inflammatory?"

"You give her what she wants, then if you insist on one of the regular drugs, maybe you can prescribe it after she's come to trust you."

"Which will be when hell freezes over," he snapped.

"Probably. But she's reasonable. All the people here are reasonable, which is why, when malaria hit, they took quinine—"

"Quinine?" he interrupted. "Isn't that pretty old-school treatment for malaria?"

"Been around for hundreds of years, but it's cheap, and it works. And it's what I was able to get the pharmaceutical companies to donate to me."

"Seriously?"

She nodded. "That's the way it works here, Justin. For the most part we get donated drugs, prescriptions that have gone over the expiration date but are still good, partial prescriptions that haven't all been taken. And quinine worked just fine for us. But I used it along with Eula's prescribed water and orange juice fast, along with warm-water cleanses. It all worked together, and who's to say which was more effective—the natural remedy or the quinine, which is actually a natural remedy itself."

"So what you're telling me is that patience with the people here will be a virtue."

"My husband always said patience is more than a virtue, it's a necessity. But he was the most patient man to ever grace the earth." She smiled fondly. "Which was good, because I'm not and I needed that counterbalance."

"Then I say your husband deserves an award, because there aren't too many patient people around."

"He did deserve an award," she said. "For a lot more than his patience. Landry was a good man. Maybe the best man I'll ever know."

She was speaking of him in the past tense, but Justin hated to ask, because if she was widowed, that was something he should have read on her application for working with his grandmother. Truth was, he'd hardly read past her name and credentials, he had been so impatient to hire someone. "And you're not…" He glanced down at her wedding ring.

"Not moving on, like most people think I should. But I don't have to. Landry can't be replaced, and I don't particularly want to."

"How long?" he asked.

"A little over two years. Leonie was just a baby when he was diagnosed, and he didn't get to stay with us very long after that. It was a pervasive pancreatic cancer. Took him almost before he knew he was sick. And you know what? If I'd known your grandmother then, I'd have been happy to give her herbal treatments a try, because I was desperate for anything. To try anything that might save him."

"I'm so sorry," Justin said.

"So am I, every day of my life. But thank you for the sentiment."

"You're raising your daughter by yourself?"

"Yes, but I have a supportive family—mother, father, six sisters. They're so much help to me, and they love Leonie. You might have heard of my mother, actually. Zenobia."

Justin blinked hard. "Seriously? Dr. Doucet is your mother? I've heard her lecture. She's…extraordinary."

"I think so. As a mother, anyway. As a doctor, I know she has her reputation, but I don't pay much attention to that. So now, about Miss Willie…" Mellette pulled a small jar out of the pocket of her tan cargo pants and handed it to him. "I'd suggest you take this to her and try to make amends. I'm with you on getting her an anti-inflammatory prescription since I've been noting some gradual changes in her physicality, but in the year I've worked here she's refused every time I've mentioned it. Maybe if you can get on her good side…"

He laughed out loud. "Do you really think that's going to happen?"

"No. But I don't believe in giving up."

He tucked the jar of liniment into his pocket, then went back to the stove to stir the gumbo. "I'm serious about wanting you to add an extra day to your schedule here."

"And I'm serious about not having the time. I work full time in emergency at New Hope, and between that and this, there's no more time to give you. As it is, you're getting my two days off from the hospital every week."

"What about working here full time?" he asked, not sure where that had come from. Certainly, he could afford her. But he wasn't sure he wanted to.

"You don't mean that."

"Actually, I might."

"You'd have to match, maybe even exceed my entire salary from the hospital, depending on how many hours you'd want me to work here, plus make up the difference for what you're paying me when I'm here. And you'd have to cover my benefits—insurance, retirement plan, paid holiday. I'm a pretty well-paid specialist, Doctor, and I really don't think I'm the solution for whatever you're trying to accomplish."

"What I'm trying to accomplish is to offer this community more medical care than they currently have. My grandmother loved these people, and taking care of them is what she would have wanted me to do."

"Then stay and take care of them."

"Not a chance."

She smiled. "Eula said you were too good for the likes of Big Swamp. Although I think she secretly believed you'd come back to it someday."

"I'm not too good for Big Swamp. I might have thought that at one time, but I grew up. But I do have a life that doesn't include mosquitoes, muskrats and alligators, and it's a life I enjoy."

"I have a life I enjoy, too, and if I don't get back to my patients, I'm not going to get home to that life tonight." Mellette headed for the door, then spun around to face him before she went back to the room full of waiting patients. "Your grandma was proud of the work you do, Justin. *My grandson, the real doctor,* is what she always used to say. For what it's worth, I don't think she ever resented the fact that you chose the city over her."

In the city… Yes, that was where he belonged. But lately he wasn't sure why. In fact, the only thing he was sure of at the moment was that hiring Mellette had been one of the best things he'd done in a long, long time. Now all he had to do was convince her to take over here full time. Maybe then his guilty feelings would be assuaged. Or some of them.

The day went surprisingly fast, and while the patients weren't flocking to Justin, the handful he did manage to see turned out to be a big help to her. So now Mellette could get out of Big Swamp before dark and make it back to Leonie before bedtime, for which she was eternally grateful. "You going to work again tomorrow?" she asked him, as she dipped a spoon into the gumbo that had been simmering for the better part of the day.

"If you want to call it working. I saw four people, and got rejected by four people."

"But they gave you a chance, and that's almost as good as them letting you treat them. Good gumbo, by the way. I think you inherited Eula's cooking talents."

"That was one of the things I always took for granted, I think. She had an amazing way in the kitchen that I didn't appreciate until I was away from here, living on fast food and whatever else I could scrounge cheaply."

"Well, if you should ever decide to give up medicine, I can definitely see you in a restaurant kitchen."

"I'd invite you to stay, except I know you want to get back to your daughter."

"And I might have taken you up on the offer, but you're right. I need some time with her—don't get enough of it." Heading toward the door, she paused before she stepped outside. "Did you ever take that liniment to Miss Willie?" she asked. "Because if you didn't, I'm betting now would be a good time. And I think she'd appreciate the gumbo, too. She doesn't do much cooking for herself these days, and a nice, hearty meal would do her some good."

"As much good as it would do me, getting into her good graces?"

"Every little bit helps," she quipped. "Oh, and I think she probably likes her gumbo over rice."

"Can you point me in the direction of her house?" he asked. "I might have known once, but it's been a long time since I've gone tromping through this backcountry, and I don't particularly like the idea of getting lost out there this time of day."

"I can do you better than pointing. I'm going to go right by her place. I can give you a lift, and that should be good enough to show you how to get yourself back before the sun goes down."

It didn't take a minute for Justin to ladle out enough gumbo for several meals into one bowl, and scoop up an ample amount of rice into another. "Who would have ever guessed I'd be making house calls and carrying in food," he said, shutting the kitchen door behind him, then following Mellette down to the boat dock where her skiff was moored.

It was a small boat but big enough to seat four comfortably. Not fast, but high enough to sit her above the reach of alligators and other water creatures that might get curious. Not that an alligator had ever come near enough to threaten her. But she was a city girl after all. And even though her city sat on the edge of Big Swamp, that didn't mean she had swamp experience. In fact, she'd surprised herself taking this part-time job where she had to boat in and out for easiest access, dodging stumps and roots. There'd been any number of part-time opportunities available at New Hope, or in other private enterprises, but something about the call of the wild had intrigued her.

Maybe it had been Landry's influence. He'd loved Big Swamp. Had spent part of his childhood in a community not too far from here. Being here made her feel closer to him.

"Who'd have ever thought you'd get me out on the bayou in a boat, all by myself, just to get to work?" she countered, as she took her seat and started the engine. "But never say never, right?"

"Being a Doucet, I guess this really wouldn't be normal for you, would it?" he said, setting down the bowls of food in the bottom of the boat.

"Being a Doucet, nothing's normal. We're an… I guess the best way you can put it is an unusual family. Seven girls… My poor daddy. I know he wanted a son, but he turned out to be quite prodigious in the daughter department. And at times I think it simply overwhelmed him. Then he held out such high hopes for a grandson when I was pregnant, and got another girl."

"Whom he loves, I'm sure," Justin said, sitting back as the thrum of the boat's engine settled into a gentle cadence while they wound their way through Big Swamp trees.

"He adores her. In fact, Daddy's retired now—he was an anesthesiologist—and he's the one who watches Leonie most of the time. Spoils her rotten. But I do hope that someday one of my sisters gives him a grandson."

"Leonie's his only grandchild?"

"So far. I'm the only one who's married. My sisters Sabine and Delphine, twins, are dedicated doctors, and Magnolia's a legal medical investigator. Then there are Ghislaine, Lisette and Acadia, all of them in various stages of their medical education or careers." She smiled. "We're close in age. My mother didn't want to interrupt her medical career for too long, so she popped us all out pretty quickly, about a year apart. And so far I'm the only one to take the marriage plunge. But it's Daddy's biggest fear that the rest of them will fall in love at the same time and he'll have to spring for six weddings in rapid succession."

"I can't even imagine having that many brothers or sisters," he said.

"Eula never really told me much about your family situation."

"There wasn't much to tell. I was an only child. Didn't come from Big Swamp, although my father did, obviously, as Eula was his mother. But my grandfather took my dad out of here when he left my grandmother to seek fame and fortune or whatever it is he wanted to do, and never looked back. He pretty much poisoned my dad to Big Swamp, and the people who lived here. Including my grandmother. Anyway, my parents raised me in New Orleans, then after they were killed—plane crash—I ended up with my grandmother in the place where my dad had refused to go."

"And you forever hated it here?"

"That's what she told you?"

"Not in so many words, but it makes sense. You left here when you were a kid, hardly ever came back to see her. Probably under your father's influence in some remote way. It only stands to reason that you didn't want to be here, given the history. Still don't, I suppose." She steered around a clump of low-hanging moss, then slowed down as a meandering nutria swam by the boat, not at all concerned about being disturbed. It was his domain, she supposed, and he was simply asserting his place in it.

"Still don't on a permanent basis, but I've been

back plenty of times to visit my grandmother," he said, but without much conviction in his voice. "Look, earlier when you said we need to talk… you're right. I really do want to sit down and talk to you about what I'm going to do here to take care of these people."

"Why do you care?" she asked as she veered to the left and puttered her way up a shallow inlet.

"Because my grandmother cared."

"Then that leads me to the obvious question."

"Let me save you the trouble of asking. The reason I didn't move back here, not even to New Orleans, to be closer is…complicated, and I'm not even sure I can explain it to myself, let alone someone else. It's just the way things were with me. I ended up in Chicago, liked it and stayed. And, yes, I did have opportunities here. Could have gone to New Hope, actually. But coming back here, being so close…" He shrugged. "I like my practice, like Chicago. Like the life I have there."

"And you were afraid that coming back to Big

Swamp, even for visits, would overwhelm you with all kinds of guilty feelings."

She slowed the boat alongside a rickety old dock, then pointed to a shanty about two hundred feet off the water. It was wooden, painted red, with blue shutters. All the paint chipped and faded. In the yard lay three good-size alligators, looking lazy and not particularly interested in the meddlers coming around to bother them.

"Or I was afraid that coming back to Big Swamp would overwhelm me with all kinds of responsibilities I can't handle. Which is turning out to be the case."

"Look, I'm not working tomorrow evening. If you can get to town, come by the house for dinner, around seven. Not sure you'll want to travel these parts at night to get home, so you're invited to stay. It'll be at my parents' house, by the way. I don't live with them, but I'm sure they'll be more than happy to extend their hospitality. That is, if you make it through the gators tonight."

"And just how am I supposed to do that?"

"Very carefully," she said, handing him one

of his bowls of food. "They have short legs, so I think you'll be able to outrun them." She laughed. "But they do have that one fast burst of energy at the start, so if you don't make it to dinner tomorrow night, I'll know what happened."

CHAPTER THREE

AS THE DAY dragged on, Justin found himself more and more anxious to go to town and have dinner with Mellette and her family. It was a kind invitation, and the idea of being around real medical people again excited him because the longer he was away from his practice the more he missed it. The most appealing part of the evening, though, was the prospect of getting to know Mellette. Even though she'd made it perfectly clear she wasn't ready to move on from her husband.

All that was fine with him, as there was no time in his life for a relationship outside a professional one. He had too much ambition wrapped up in his fast rise to where he was, and that was important to him. Maybe the most important thing. Not that he had anything in mind for Mellette other than trying to convince her to work in Big Swamp full time. Because he didn't. She was his means to an end—he hoped. The person who could put things right for a lot of people. Himself included.

And he'd done some predawn soul-searching on just how to accomplish what he needed. Tried coming up with an incentive that would work for everyone involved, but especially for Mellette, because he wanted to make this offer something that would benefit her in ways that mattered. So by the time dawn began to awaken the bayou, and all the otters and raccoons outside were taking their first morning stretches, he was fairly certain he'd hit upon the perfect plan.

Although he wasn't convinced enough to be smug about it, since he was fully aware that what he was about to offer Mellette could well fly in the face of her close-knit family and cause some blaring divisions there. Big life changes had a way of making that happen—something he knew from firsthand experience.

Still, he was keeping his fingers crossed that this plan would work out; the more he thought about it, the more he knew Mellette was his only strong answer. And a strong answer was the only thing that could work, owing to all the obstacles Big Swamp presented.

"I'm working on the book," Justin told his literary agent in a just-after-dawn phone call. "But I'm pretty busy here, taking care of all my grandmother's unfinished business." Well, that wasn't exactly as true as it should have been, as he hadn't even begun to tie up loose ends. But he *was* working on a plan to open a clinic, and it was his intention to get all the personal matters tied up in the next couple of weeks so he wasn't exactly lying. Just jumping the gun on his to-do list.

"You're not going to blow your deadline, are you, Justin? Because if you are, I need to get it squared away with your editor."

Deadlines, editor… Yes, he kept himself almost as busy writing as he did being a doctor these days. Truth was, he enjoyed his growing passion for being a medical mystery novelist. It had happened quite by accident, when he'd been asked to step in at the last minute to consult on the medical aspect of a movie being filmed in Chicago. A couple more movie and television gigs had come from that, along with the idea of writing a novel.

And while Justin hadn't been an overnight best-selling author, his career was promising enough to get him his first two-book contract for starters. Now he was on his second two-book contract, and there were faint whispers of turning his second book into a movie. It was a long shot, but exciting.

He liked writing. Didn't want to stop doing it. But he didn't know how it was going to fit into his long-term plans, because his medical practice really did take up more time than he'd ever thought it would. So that was his career crisis. How could he manage all aspects of it? Or how could he separate out the aspects he wanted to prioritize?

What he could figure out, though, was that he was staying in Big Swamp much longer than he'd expected to—it was at least giving him more time to write, to edit, to work up to that next deadline, even though he'd been brain-dead the past few days, putting off the decisions he'd have to make eventually. Putting off life in general. Also, there was something about the surroundings here that was conducive to his story setting, so much eerie nature that was a real kick to his creative mystery-writing process.

He liked that, liked the mood the Big Swamp ambiance put him in when he did write. The bayou and all its shadows and swamp creatures, the wild moss dropping down from everywhere, the sounds, the smells… "I don't need a deadline extension," he told his agent. "Except for a few days of sluggishness trying to figure out what I'm going to do with this place, it's been good here. So you'll probably get this book a couple weeks early for a change."

Normally, owing to his Chicago schedule, he was a couple of weeks late, sometimes more, because every aspect of his hectic life kept him on edge, aware of every minute ticking off on the clock. Unlike Louisiana, where he lost hours, immersed in his work. So in that respect Big Swamp was being very good to him. Good juju, his grandma would have said. Meaning Big Swamp brought him good luck or good fortune.

In the end, that wasn't going to matter since he was going back to Chicago just as soon as he had the clinic situation straightened out. Why leave when Big Swamp agreed with him? Maybe because hectic agreed with him more. Or maybe because hectic was his habit. Either way, it didn't matter. He wasn't staying here.

So after his chat with his agent, and as Justin settled down by the window to edit his latest novel, he caught himself gazing outside more than he should. Distracted. Wondering if someone from the community in need of medical attention might stop by to see him. Fretting a little because they didn't.

It was odd how that need was coming through loud and strong, because until this very morning, this very instant, he'd had no idea he'd harbored these feelings of wanting to help out personally here. It was strange to discover it, and he didn't understand it. So why exactly did he want to see patients who obviously didn't want to see him? Was it to assuage his guilty feelings over his grandmother? Or to do the right thing by the people here, the thing his grandmother would have wanted? Maybe even expected from him?

Then the oddest of all possibilities struck him. *Would this have anything to do with impressing Mellette?*

No, he was ruling that one out. She was strictly a hands-off lady who didn't want to be impressed by any man. While she definitely brought out some manly instinct in him, he was going to respect her wishes. Keep his distance. Let her stay married to her deceased husband for as long as she needed.

In which case…that meant this melancholia had to be because he was disappointed by how not one single person had stopped by. And here he was, ready to treat anything—a head cold, a hangnail, even a bug bite.

So rather than treating patients, he spent the morning editing, going back over the minute details that were so important to his brand, not to mention his reputation, checking his spelling, making sure all his periods, commas and ellipses were in the right place. All this while alternately gazing out the window then chastising himself for being distracted by things that would never happen.

But it did distract him that people deliberately avoided him…distracted him so much that he eventually gave himself over to a walk that took him down to the water's edge, where he tossed some stale bread to a fat little duck that had come begging. After that, he even spent a few extra minutes strolling along the riverbank, then down the road, hoping to see someone, hoping someone would see him. But nothing. Not a single, solitary medical thing occurred. In fact, he couldn't be sure but he felt as if he was being deliberately avoided; he didn't encounter anybody on a walk that took him almost all the way in to Grandmaison, which was a good three miles.

It sure wasn't a good feeling, not being needed by the people here. But then, he hadn't really put himself out there to let anybody know he was available, had he? Or that he wanted to be needed.

Of course, had they known, they still wouldn't have come. That was something about which he was reasonably sure. But was there some way to change their perception of him?

The bigger question, though, was why he wanted the bother. Why did it matter? Why should he care? "Because she's getting to you," he said as he kicked a stone along the road on his way back home. "You're a schoolboy, trying to impress a little girl." Pull her pigtails. Tease her until she runs home to tell her mother. Treat her patients to show her what a good doctor he was. It was all the same. He *was* a schoolboy trying to impress a girl…a girl who didn't want to be impressed. "Well, I'll be damned…" he said, as he checked his watch to see how many hours it was until his dinner date with Mellette's family. "I'll be double dogged damned."

Mellette's advice had been to prove himself by simply being a doctor to the people here, which had flopped badly. Even his attempt at liniment and make-up gumbo for Miss Willie had been received badly. She'd accepted it, given him an icy thank-you and shut the door on him with a final-sounding *thunk.*

"So what am I supposed to do?" he asked Napoleon once he was back on his front porch, laptop in position, ready to get back to his book. The tomcat, who was stretched out on the windowsill, taking in the afternoon sun, didn't show the least bit of concern. "And why do I even care? That's the real question. Why do I care? I mean, it's not like I'm going to stay here and put myself into this culture again." Not that he'd ever really been a part of it when he'd lived here. He'd been the outsider who'd never wanted to fit in.

So wanting to fit in now was the furthest thing from his mind. But he did feel the obligations left by his grandmother tugging at him. And maybe that was the real kicker. The more he didn't want to feel anything, the more he felt. Right now, he felt strongly that he couldn't let his grandmother down this one last time. There were so many things in his life that couldn't be undone, so many regrets it was too late to make right. The way he'd refused to help his grandmother was probably the biggest regret of all, because he'd lost that final time with her.

Now he lost sleep over it. He'd dropped ten pounds, too, and gained a new crease in his forehead. "But I didn't know," he said to Napoleon. "Why didn't she…why didn't *someone* tell me, even though she didn't want them to?" Even Mellette. Why hadn't she picked up the phone? One phone call. One lousy phone call.

He sighed, cursing the thought of his grandmother here alone, dying, swiping back the tears that always came when he thought about it. "She should have told me, Napoleon. I know she thought it was for my own good. That I was too busy or too important to come home… How did I ever let something like that happen?" His voice went quiet. "How did I ever let her down so much when all she did was love me?"

There was nothing to add, nothing to say. They kept to themselves, these people. Kept to themselves and shut him out. Letting out a long, anguished breath, he said, “So here I am, Napoleon. Basking in the sun like you, regretting the whole blasted mess. Wanting to change something that can’t be changed.” He reached through the open window and scratched the cat behind his ears. “I supposed I should be glad your life is working out better than mine. At least people around here respond to you.”

Napoleon’s response was to hop down out of the window, stick his tail in the air and walk away.

“You hate me, too?” he called after the haughty cat, then stretched back in his desk chair, trying hard to focus again on the page on his screen. The one where the heroine had just discovered the medication switch and was hoping she wasn’t too late to save the life of the gallant and heroic young doctor. Ironic how it paralleled his life in a way, he thought as he deleted an entire page where the heroine seemed to be going in circles. Wasn’t he himself running in circles, too late to take care of the things that were important to him? And he was the only one to blame.

By midafternoon Justin had finally put aside his distractions enough to allow the creative juices to flow, and they were flowing so effusively he nearly forgot about his dinner appointment. So by the time he grabbed a quick shower, changed into a pair of khaki cargos and a white cotton shirt, then climbed into his grandmother's thirty-year-old pickup truck, he was wondering if he should simply bow out since he was going to be so late. Instead, he hit the back roads at speeds much faster than were really safe and got himself into New Orleans only fifteen minutes late.

By the time he was knocking at the Doucet mansion front door he was nearly winded, not from the rush of getting there but from the nervousness of what the evening ahead could mean to him.

"Thought one of those gators might have gotten you," Mellette said, opening the door to him.

"No such luck," he said, entering the foyer to

what had to be one of the grandest homes he'd ever stepped foot in. Just the foyer was lavish with French antiques—at least he thought they were French, as he truly didn't know one antique from another. There were mirrors and gold knickknacks. An ornate gold clock with fat little cherubs sitting on its base and a crystal chandelier that was so grand it overshadowed everything else in the space. He wondered how on earth it was ever cleaned since all the ceiling lamps in his condo were single white globes that dusted easily with a swipe or two.

Everything he could see from his vantage point at the front door dripped with elegance, and the doctor who normally lived pretty high-end himself was suddenly self-conscious about his casual outfit. He should have known better. No, he *did* know better. "I, um…I'm not really dressed for dinner," he said when he realized how beautifully Mellette was dressed. She wore a sleeveless mid-calf floral-print dress that flowed on forever. And gold sandals. She had on just a hint of makeup and a large red hibiscus over her left ear. The one word that came to mind when he set eyes on her was *stunning.* Followed by another word of warning: *off-limits.*

"You're fine," she said. "We don't dress formally. Not with the hectic lives we all live."

"But look at you," he said. "Then look at me. One of us here isn't dressed right, and I'm guessing it's me."

She smiled. "At work I'm either in scrubs or cargo pants and a T-shirt. Sometimes it's nice to get dressed up a little bit."

Actually, those cargo pants and that T-shirt looked pretty good on her, too. "Well, I hope you didn't wait on my account. I lost track of the time…"

She laughed. "Don't flatter yourself. When my daddy decides it's time to sit down and eat, we sit down and eat. The only one he waits for is my mother, who's not here yet. But she called, and she's about fifteen minutes out."

"Would that be enough time for me to run out and buy a proper suit?" he asked.

"That would be enough time for you to meet

my daddy and my daughter. My sisters Sabine, Delphine and Magnolia—we call her Maggie—will also be having dinner with us, and they're upstairs, getting ready."

"I'm the only guest?" he asked, quite surprised.

"The only one."

"Talk about making an underdressed guy feel self-conscious."

"My family's normal, Justin. We can be as mean as swamp gators when we have to be—and that's usually to defend the family—but most of the time we're just like anybody else."

"And if I could identify one antique from another, would all this glitz and glamour around me say the same thing?"

"Family heirlooms. My great-grandmother on my mother's side decorated this house, and there's never really been a need to change anything. We like the family tradition. But I thought you had a nice lifestyle going back in Chicago. Your grandmother told me you live pretty well there."

"I do. But it's…well, not this. I keep my space sparse and scaled back."

"Eula told me about your fast cars and even faster women. She said you have quite a reputation for that."

"My grandmother had a big imagination and maybe a few high hopes, because that's not my life at all. I own a nice little European sports car and a larger car for when it snows. But as far as my women…" He smiled. "Between you and me, I haven't had a date in over a year, and the last woman I dated was fast, but not in the way you'd think."

Mellette raised her eyebrows in surprise. "Seriously? No girlfriends? From what Eula described, it sounded like you have a revolving door on your condo."

"Taking some time off. Between my medical practice, which is growing, and… You know about my writing, don't you?"

"I may have read one of your books," she admitted.

"Well, that's my life. All of it. No time left over

for anything else except a few hours' sleep every night. Sometimes not even that by the time I get everything done." His eyes traveled to the miniature version of Mellette who was being escorted down the front staircase by a distinguished, gray-haired man Justin assumed to be Mellette's father.

She was a stunning child, and identical to Mellette in every way except she had long, flowing black hair, whereas Mellette's was cropped short. They were even dressed alike, same floral print, same gold sandals. He was a man who didn't normally pay too much attention to children, but Leonie was adorable. His first thought went to Landry, and he felt an unusual tug of sadness that the man would never know his daughter. His second thought went to Mellette, who beamed with pure love when she took her daughter's hand.

"This is Leonie," she said, quite simply. Then to Leonie, "This is Dr. Bergeron."

Leonie thrust her tiny hand out to shake his. "Hello," she said, in a voice that seemed deep for a child so young. “Are you my mommy’s friend?” she asked.

“This is the man for whom I work for when I go to Big Swamp, *ma chère,*” Mellette explained.

“I thought you worked for Bonne-Maman Eula,” Leonie said seriously.

“I did. But remember how I told you that Bonne-Maman Eula died?”

Leonie nodded. “And went to heaven, like Daddy did.”

“Well, this is Bonne-Maman Eula’s grandson, just like you are Grandpère Charles’s granddaughter.”

“Then you’re the new doctor,” Leonie said.

“I’m the very new doctor,” Justin replied. He turned to Mellette. “She’s well-spoken for her age.”

“We’ve noticed that,” Mellette said, smiling at the compliment. “We figure at the rate she’s going, she’ll be taking over the medical center for my mother in the next decade or so.”

“Days like this and I’m ready to have her take over right now,” Zenobia Doucet said, coming in the front door. She was a stately woman. Tall, like Mellette. But with honey-colored hair, which she wore pulled tightly back from her face to reveal flawless bone structure. Zenobia was the kind of woman whose looks belied her age—she could have been forty, she could have been seventy. There was no way of telling.

"Bad day, Maman?" Mellette asked.

"One of those days that make me wish I was involved in patient care again and not working as an administrator." Zenobia dropped her purse and scarf on a bench by the door and immediately went to pick up her granddaughter. "So if anybody has a problem tonight, please, keep it to yourself. I've solved everything from a missing paper-towel shipment to an overbooked O.R., and for the next twelve hours I need a clear head." She turned to Justin and smiled. "And you must be our guest for the night. So pleased you could join us, Dr. Bergeron."

"Actually, just a dinner guest. I was raised in the swamp so I don't have a fear of negotiating it at night."

"With alligators?" Leonie asked.

"Great big ones," Justin said. "With great big eyes that glow in the dark."

"Anybody care for a glass of wine or fruit juice before dinner?" Charles asked. Then he smiled at Justin. "Full bar, my boy. Anything you like."

"Beer?" he ventured.

Charles laughed. "You're a man after my own heart. One beer coming up. Actually, I think I'll join you."

"I want apple juice," Leonie announced.

"And apple juice it will be," Charles said, taking his granddaughter back from Zenobia and heading off to the kitchen with her.

"As you can see, my parents spoil my daughter," Mellette said.

"That's what grandchildren are for," Zenobia said, then scooted around Justin. "Please, Dr. Bergeron, make yourself at home. I'm going to go get ready for dinner, so whatever you need until then, please ask Mellette. Or Charles, if you can pry him away from Leonie long enough." With that she flounced up the stairs with surprising energy, leaving Justin and Mellette alone in the foyer.

"Sorry it's so hectic," Mellette said, showing Justin through the house to the veranda out back, stopping briefly as Charles appeared with a bottle of beer for Justin and a glass of sparkling water for her.

"You don't drink?" Justin asked, again feeling self-conscious.

Mellette shook her head. "One of my sisters had a problem for a short time, and while my other sisters and I helped her recover, we..." She shrugged. "It's just a personal preference. My mother likes her evening sherry and my dad likes a good, stiff whiskey. Or, apparently, a bottle of beer."

"And I feel like a real slump. Will probably feel more so when your sisters come down to dinner and are dressed as beautifully as you are."

"We don't stand on formality, Justin. If we did, I would have told you. In fact, when we were growing up we hardly ever sat down together for a meal, we were always so busy."

"My grandmother always insisted we eat together. When I was younger it wasn't so bad, but the older I got the more I resented the intrusion in my life. She never relented, though, and now I'm glad she didn't. Those were good times."

"And your parents?"

He shrugged. "They weren't really a major factor in my upbringing. Both of them worked all the time, traveled with a major oil company, and I hardly ever saw them." He took a swig of his beer, then set the bottle down on the cement wall where they seated themselves. "My grandmother was my influence."

"I know," she said quietly. "And you were lucky to have her. She was an amazing woman."

"Why didn't you call me when she got sick? I know she didn't want you to, but why didn't you, out of courtesy? Or even obligation to the man who signed your paycheck?"

Mellette hesitated, then frowned. "I wanted to. But like you said, she didn't want me to. Said you were too busy, that your work was too important to interrupt."

"You should have called, anyway. I would have come."

"And disrespected her wishes?"

"And given me a little final time with her."

"She wasn't that sick, Justin. I mean, in that, she wasn't being very truthful with me because I'm pretty sure she knew how badly off she was. But she just wasn't letting on to anyone. Not me, not Amos…

"In fact, she never took to her bed until her very last day. She was feeling tired, but that's all. At least, that's what she was telling me. And she was working through the malaria outbreak, treating people right and left. Then she just… If she'd told me how she was *really* feeling, I would have called you no matter what she wanted. Would have gotten her into a hospital, too. But Eula was literally on her feet until the day before she died, and she got pretty fiery when I mentioned calling you."

"I should have known, though. Somebody should have—"

"And I'm sorry," she said, laying a gentle hand

on his arm. "You'll never know how sorry I am, but I had no way of knowing how bad—"

"Because that's the way she was." He smiled fondly. "She always did things her way, and I guess even at the end she did what she wanted to do. I just wish…"

"So do I," she said sadly. "You don't know how often I've thought about how it turned out. The people who'd known Eula all their lives might have guessed she was sicker than she was letting on, but I'm not even sure about that." She looked over at Justin. "My husband did the same thing. He could have taken more drugs to prolong his life another month or two, but the drugs made him so groggy, and he fought so hard to stay alert. The doctors wanted him in a hospice, he wanted to stay home, which is what he did. In the end, he died the way he wanted to, just like Eula, and I don't think that's a bad thing.

"I mean, I would have loved having Landry around for another couple of months. There were so many things we didn't get to finish, and two more months…" She batted back a tear. "But it wasn't meant to be."

"We all make our choices, don't we?" He picked up his beer and took another swig.

"That's the way it should be, I think. I'm sorry you didn't get to have that final time with Eula, but she really didn't give that final time to anyone. An hour before she died she was giving me orders on how to take care of certain patients."

"You know she wanted me to come home and do my *doctoring* here, don't you? She'd asked me several times over the years…or not asked so much as suggested it could work for me, coming back to Louisiana to work."

Mellette nodded, but didn't say anything.

"That's the hard one to deal with. Because I had my life and I didn't want to change it. I got out when I was a kid, and it was never my intention to return. Sure, I could have. It would have been easy enough. But coming back… There was nothing here for me."

"She understood why you didn't. And respected you for your dedication. She had that same dedication, Justin, so she knew what it was about."

"Maybe she did, but that doesn't make me feel any better about a lot of things. Like I shouldn't have run away when I was a kid, and I should have come to visit more often than I did."

"We all have those should-haves and shouldn't-haves, don't we? But there's nothing we can do about them except maybe feel regret."

"Does the regret ever go away, though?" he asked.

"Probably not, but it mellows in time. The edges of my regrets aren't as sharp as they were when Landry died. Of course, I think part of that is because I've had to force myself to stand away from those regrets in order to keep moving forward. Life got tough, and I don't have the time, or the energy, to keep dwelling on them."

"How so?"

"I lost everything when Landry died. Not just my husband but my life's savings, my house, my car—the cost of cancer."

"Your parents didn't help?"

"They wanted to, and my parents fought me every step of the way when I refused. But I made one of those choices you just talked about."

For June, the night was quite warm, but not humid, and the cacophony of nature—frogs, crickets, all varieties of small animals—was so loud it was like an orchestrated symphony. An intricate tune composed of notes that didn't quite harmonize but still somehow fit together in their blend. "Which would have something to do with why you're not living here with them, I'm guessing?"

"They wanted me to move home." She paused, swallowed. "Begged me. Did all but drag me here. But Leonie and I need to be separate. And don't get me wrong. My family is wonderful. I love them dearly and how they want to help me means everything. But I need to establish my own family, with our own traditions and craziness, and that won't happen here, under their roof. Landry and I had very specific goals for our daughter, and part of that was helping her to become independent. So if I moved home…"

"Your parents wouldn't let you be independent."

"All done with the best intentions," she said. "But you're right. And you saw how they are with Leonie. My sisters, too. Everybody dotes on her. Spoils her rotten. Which is fine for short periods of time, but not every day, all day, the way it would be if we lived here."

"Then it sounds to me as if you're doing the right thing," he said.

"Do you think so? Because it's so difficult, and there are times when I wonder if I should give in, just for a year or two. Let them take care of me. Maybe even let them pay off the debt.

"Yet when I get down and almost give in, I just remind myself I'm doing what's right by being the best example for my daughter that I can be. You know, showing her how to be the kind of person Landry and I wanted her to be."

"He was a lucky man to have you," Justin said.

"I was the lucky one."

"Lucky, but living a tough life."

"A tough life that'll get better. I've got about another year, maybe a year and a half, then I'll be out from under the debt, and Leonie and I can start moving forward."

"Until then?"

"Until then, I work hard and my daddy gets to escort her around the house like she's a little princess."

"What if I could afford to meet all your demands? That, and figure out some way where you could bring her to work with you a day or two each week?"

"What?"

"I've been doing a lot of thinking about this, and I've decided I'd like to open up a regular clinic in Big Swamp. Something to honor my grandmother. She gave the people attention whenever they needed it, and while we're not going to be able to staff a clinic twenty-four hours a day, seven days a week, for some time to come, if ever, we could give them regular medical care five days a week for starters. Then expand as there's a need, or as we're able."

"Seriously?" she asked.

"Seriously. The thing is, you could work regular hours and go home every day at a decent time. And the best part is I've figured out a way you could bring Leonie to work occasionally. Back at my hospital in Chicago there's a child-care center, and that's maybe the biggest draw for recruiting the best medical personnel. So I'm thinking we could do something like that for Leonie right here. You know, like build a safe, fenced-in play yard for her. Find one of the local women to look after her when you're with patients. Schedule one or two light days each week so you could bring her to work and spend more time with her."

"Bring Leonie to Big Swamp…" Mellette murmured thoughtfully.

"It's just an idea. If you can think of something better…"

"It kind of scares me." She smiled. "Kind of intrigues me, too."

"So you're not ruling it out. I'm still in the running to convince you."

"No, I'm not ruling it out. Not yet. But..." She shrugged. "It's a generous offer, Justin. Generous to me, generous to the people your grandmother cared for. But you and I don't agree on the type of medicine I'd want to practice there, and that's the first problem. The second is, to have a real clinic I need something other than Eula's house to work from. Unless you're willing to convert her house into a real clinic. Then there's my family. I'm not sure how they'd take it if I quit my full-time job at New Hope to open a clinic in the bayou where I'll be dispensing herbs as much as I will medicine.

"And there's the obvious problem of my being a registered nurse who needs a physician as a medical director. I'm allowed to work unsupervised, obviously, but to make this a real clinic I need someone local to sign off as my doctor. And having you living in Chicago, as the legal owner, won't work."

"Who's doing that now?"

"No one, because it's not a licensed clinic. And when I need a prescription I can't do myself, I work it out through the hospital. But I haven't even had to do that a lot because the people in the bayou don't want traditional medicine. The thing is, I'm assuming you're going to want the emphasis of this clinic to be traditional medicine—"

"I haven't thought it through that far," he interrupted.

"Then you need to think some more, because if you build it, they're not going to come if you're only handing out pills. It has to be swamp cures and pills."

"So where does that leave us?"

"Honestly, when you first talked to me about spending more time there, then came up with the full-time offer, I didn't take you seriously because it all seemed improbable."

"Improbable or not, I'm dead serious about this."

"I know you are, and Eula would have been so pleased. I do need to think about it, though, and figure out how changing my life so drastically will affect both Leonie and me. And also the rest of my family. They're a part of this, as well."

"What about your family?" Charles asked from the doorway.

"Justin's made me an offer to come and work for him in Big Swamp."

"If I'm not mistaken, you already do work for him in Big Swamp."

"Two days a week, Daddy. But this would be more. He wants to open up a clinic there and let me run it. As in a full-time position."

Charles chuckled. "Mellette Priscilla Doucet Chaisson, swamp nurse. It has a certain ring to it. Can't say I like the sound of it, though."

"It gives me an opportunity, Daddy."

"A good one, I'm assuming."

"It will let me work fewer hours and spend more time with Leonie."

"Which will deprive me of my granddaughter throughout the day? That doesn't sound so good to me."

"Well, I haven't said yes," she told her father.

"But you haven't turned it down, have you?"

Mellette looked at Justin. "No, I haven't turned it down. Right now, I'm calling it a definite maybe."

"You do know your mother's going to want to put in a counteroffer to his offer," Charles said.

"But she can't magically produce some of the advantages Justin is offering me. Day care for Leonie, for example. New Hope doesn't have it for its employees. Also, I'll be working less hours for more money, and while I know that Mother would like to offer more, she's bound by the New Hope rules, regulations and salary guidelines. So…" Mellette shrugged.

"See how you are," Charles said. "I turn my back on you for a minute, and look what you've gone and done."

"It could be good, Daddy," she said.

He aimed his next statement directly at Justin. "For one of my daughters it has to be better than good. You remember that, Dr. Bergeron. If you intend to create any kind of a situation for any one of my daughters, it has to be perfect or you'll be answering to me. Do you understand me, young man?

"Understood, sir."

"And if Mellette accepts this offer, also understand that I'll be coming around to inspect the facility, just to make sure it's what's best for both my daughter and granddaughter."

"You're welcome anytime, sir."

Charles gave them a curt nod, then smiled. "Dinner's ready, by the way," he said on his way back inside the house. "With the bad news you're going to be breaking to your mother, I wouldn't suggest being late to her dinner table."

"Does he know something I don't know?" Justin asked, as he escorted Mellette into the dining room.

"He knows *me,*" she said.

CHAPTER FOUR

"TELL ME WHAT you need," Justin said. He and Mellette were standing shoulder to shoulder in the front yard of Eula's house, appraising the area to see what it would take to turn it into a proper medical clinic. They were also looking at the overall condition of the place and assessing the many things it lacked.

It was an old two-story traditional house, lived in by Eula's mother, and her mother before that. Well over a hundred years planted in Big Swamp, it had weathered the years with a minimum of upkeep, and while it was sturdy, it looked tired. Its wooden clapboards needed a good coat of paint, as the last one—applied fifty years previously—had worn off, leaving the boards a rustic brown with splotches of white here and there.

The handrail on the two steps up to the wooden wrap-around porch was in serious need of some shoring up from a serious left- and right-tilting wobble. And the storm shutters, which were well worn and not decorative, were ready to be replaced by new ones. Every slat was either broken or missing altogether.

All that said, it was a clean, tidy house in spite of its rundown condition. A house that was as welcoming as the line of old handmade oak rockers sitting on the front porch, where guests, patients or anybody else who wandered by could sit for a while if they wanted to. Next to the kick line of chairs hung a swing suspended from rusty chains. That had been Eula's place to sit, especially in the evenings, when the squeak from the back and forth of the chains had seemed to be louder than during the day.

And there were flowerpots full of various herbs and flowers scattered everywhere, a worn-out mat that had welcomed more guests over the years than anyone could remember and nailed prominently over the old wooden door was a sign that read Welcome. A sign Justin had never failed to look up and read every time he entered.

Mellette stepped back from the front of the house and took a good look around to make sure she wasn't about to step on a cranky gator or some other critter that had walked, crawled or slithered up from the channel—her habit every time she walked outside.

"For starters, I need the front part of the interior gutted. The structure itself seems good enough, but I need the dividing wall between the living room and dining room removed so I can turn the area into one big waiting room and reception area. Also, the old-fashioned parlor… I'd like that to stay since it sits just off the main area. We can use it for a doctor's office. And while I can use both downstairs bedrooms as exam rooms, I'll need all the furniture out of here and replaced with something more appropriate to a clinic. Maybe give the old pieces to someone in Big Swamp who's in need.

"As for the kitchen…" She shrugged. "I suppose it can stay like it is, which will give me someplace to escape to when I'm not seeing patients, and also a place to work with the herbs.

Upstairs…I'm not sure what to do with those two bedrooms. Maybe just leave them as they are for the time being, then later convert them into hospital rooms of a sort, in case we ever have anybody who needs overnight treatment. Oh, and the back storage room… That'll make a great playroom for Leonie, because the door leading outside from it can go straight into a play yard. You still intend to build her a play yard, don't you?"

"Um…yes." He'd expected changes, but not this all-out rearranging of practically everything. In fact, somehow he'd just envisioned leaving the house pretty much as it was and having Mellette continue to work here the way she had. But apparently Mellette had other ideas on the subject. Other *big* ideas. "You know this is going to take a while…all this work you're proposing."

"That's fine. I've got time, and I'm a patient woman. Oh, and the outside of the clinic…I think white would work. I know that's a little bit traditional or old-fashioned, but a nice white building just looks the part. And I'd like a new sign…I want to call it Eula's House, if that's okay with you."

"No new sign," he said. "That welcome sign has always been there, and it stays. Not negotiable."

She arched inquisitive eyebrows at him, like she wanted to ask him a question, but instead she said, "Then it stays, and we'll have some kind of sign made that we can install in the yard."

Well, she'd gone from hard to convince to exuberant overnight. The enthusiasm was cute, he'd give her that. But the project itself? He wasn't sure if he liked or hated all the changes she was proposing. They sounded practical, and they were certainly in keeping with the clinic he'd asked her to run. But it was all so…extreme.

Justin took a few steps backward to study the house he'd been raised in and his eyes immediately went to his bedroom window. How many nights had he sneaked out that window, jumped across to the old cottonwood tree then shimmied down it to freedom? And how many times had he sneaked back in the front door, pulled off his shoes under the welcome sign so they wouldn't clack across the wooden floor, glad that by some miracle the door was unlocked, then crept back up the creaky stairs, never, ever getting caught?

Sighing, with just a tinge of regret, Justin wondered if he was making a mistake here, changing things so drastically. Or maybe his own enthusiasm was dragging because he actually did have some emotional attachment to the house that had only just now come to the surface. Fond memories of his childhood he'd shoved back to the recesses of his memory were beginning to creep their way back out.

Whatever the case, he was feeling like a great big wet blanket this morning and not even Mellette's pretty smile was enough to shake it out of him. "Do you intend keeping the clinic open during renovations?" he asked, trying to focus on the goal and not the means of achieving it.

"I'd think we have to. Even though you don't approve of most of the services we've offered, people here count on them. Also, if you insist on turning this into more of a medical facility, I'm still going to need a medical director. Someone to oversee or prescribe when I can't. That's a priority, Justin. I have some leeway because I have a master's in nursing, but not enough to do all the things I think you envision here."

He knew that, of course. And so far hadn't even gotten around to thinking about that aspect of the clinic. "Any suggestions?" he asked her.

A smile spread to her face. "Maybe one, but I'd have to do a lot of sweet-talking to convince him, and especially convince his wife."

"Who?"

"My dad. He retired much too young. Had some diabetic complications, and the doctor told him the stress of his job was contributing to his poor health. He was the head of anesthesiology at New Hope. So he decided to take some time off, and that was the same time I started needing help with Leonie. One thing led to another, he decided he liked the life of leisure, and my mother especially liked not having to worry about him so much, so he resigned from the hospital to be a stay-at-home grandpa. Which he loves.

"But I really think he misses medicine, and while clinical medicine isn't what he did in the past, I think he might be persuaded to oversee operations here, maybe even see a few patients every now and then, especially diabetic patients, if we're lucky. That's if I can convince my mother that it won't hurt him. She's pretty protective of Daddy, probably more than he needs."

"Wow. You've gone way ahead of me on all of this. I was still trying to find reasons to convince you to accept the job, and you've already turned this place into a major medical clinic with its own doctor. I'm impressed." Bowled over was more like it.

"One thing you'll discover about the Doucet family is that when we make a commitment, we follow through. Or, in some cases, plow right through. We're a pretty powerful bunch to be reckoned with."

"Then I think I should make it a point to stay on your good side."

Mellette smiled, but there was a riptide of steel

and determination in that smile. "Take those words to heart, Doctor. They'll serve you well."

Damn, but he liked her. She wasn't soft. In fact, he wasn't sure she was at all bendable. And she wasn't particularly effervescent, which was what he usually found in the women in went for. But Mellette had this untempered way about her that was, well, for a lack of a better definition, sexy. She was no-nonsense. Strong willed. Straightforward. All of it a very intriguing yet feminine package unlike anything he'd ever seen or experienced before.

But he was off women for now. Totally. He was struggling enough, managing his own life right now and holding all the pieces in place. The last thing he needed was to complicate that. A woman would definitely complicate it. The funny thing was, he was okay with that. Better than okay, really. He was downright pleased with the arrangement.

Particularly since the last one had connived her way in a little too deeply for comfort. She'd been pretty to look at but pernicious in ways that still made him shudder. So he'd promised himself some time off to re-evaluate his future. To see how he wanted to proceed, whether that be as a bachelor, which wasn't all that bad, or in a committed relationship, which, admittedly, scared him to death. He'd been there, done that and pulled off an epic fail. "Trust me, I was on a powerful woman's bad side not that long ago, and it's a place I don't want to find myself again."

"Broken heart?" she asked.

"Not even close. Her daddy was a politician and I was *chosen* to join a rather high-ranking family. It was flattering being in that company for a while, but let's just say it was a family I didn't like as much as they liked me, and I wasn't even smart enough at the time to realize just how much I didn't like them, I was so busy being flattered."

"So you have an aversion to powerful people?"

"Like your family? No. But I do I have an aversion to powerful people who use their power to corrupt. Nancy's daddy dearest sat on the hospital board, and it was his goal to terminate a charity program I was involved in.

"Why?"

"Because it didn't turn a profit."

"But you won the battle, didn't you?"

He shook his head. "Just the opposite. I sat front and center on the losing side."

"What kind of charity?"

"A recovery day camp for kids who'd undergone major physical trauma."

"They yanked the funding on that?"

He nodded. "Said there were other charities just as worthy, which is true. The hospital had only so much money available for charitable works, and it seemed that Nancy's father had a pet charity in mind ready to grab the funds from our little fledgling. The thing is, his pet wasn't bad, but he had his fingerprints all over it as a founder, and he wanted to use that to catapult him into an elected office. Anyway, our little charity was new, hadn't made much of a splash yet, and he simply got greedy for our funding and convinced the board to cut it off."

"But you stayed there at the hospital after they did that?"

"I have too many years invested there to walk away. And my general surgery practice is one of the strongest anywhere. I don't want to leave it."

"Yet you left the girlfriend?"

"Actually, I was getting ready to but she beat me to it, told me she was disappointed that I wasn't man enough to beat her daddy. That's when I realized…"

"Let me guess. She knew her daddy would be waging war with you, and she wiggled her way in to spite him. She was using you as her agenda to beat him."

"Something like that. And he used me as well, because he'd hoped the charity founders would just back away quietly and I could facilitate that because of my relationship with Nancy. He didn't want to be seen as the big, bad ogre who had killed sick kids' hopes and dreams, and I was supposed to be the one who shielded him from that. It didn't turn out that way, and he took a bad hit to his reputation because of it, was forced off the hospital board, and in the end he hated me as much as Nancy did."

"And your charity program?"

"Another hospital grabbed it and ran with it."

"Then that part's good," she said.

"That part's good, and the rest of it is… embarrassing. I should have been smarter."

"You don't equate their kind of power with us, do you?" she asked.

"No. Not at all. You come from a powerful family, but there are bad ways to handle power and good ways, and your family is an example of what's good. They prove that power doesn't have to corrupt."

"Good, because I was afraid you might think we were like Nancy's family, and—"

"Not a chance. I just look at that whole incident as a bad mistake in love."

"But we all make mistakes in love," Mellette said, almost dreamily.

"Even you?"

She nodded. "Even me. I should have married Landry years before I did. He was my one and only, but I wanted to finish my education, so I kept putting him off, figuring we had a lot of years ahead of us. As it turned out, I was wrong."

"I'm sorry for that," Justin said sincerely.

"So am I, every day of my life." Mellette's eyes misted up, but she blinked back the tears before they fell. "Anyway, back to what we're going to do here," she said, sniffling then clearing her throat.

For sure, Landry had been a lucky man having someone that fiercely devoted to him. Had he known how lucky he was? "Well, you wouldn't happen to know a general contractor who could oversee the work, would you?"

"Landry's brother is a contractor, actually. I can call him and see if he'll come out and give us an estimate, then we can…" She paused and gave him a doubtful look. "You're having second thoughts about this, aren't you?"

"Yes and no. Having the clinic here's the right thing to do, but…"

"But this was your home and it's hard letting go."

He nodded. "It's my last connection to her, and I suppose that's just beginning to hit me. It's hard to believe she's not going to come walking out that front door and tell me to get washed up for supper, that we're going to have red beans and rice and corn bread. Or that she needs a mess of crawdads for the gumbo, and to make myself useful and go catch some for her."

"Your grandmother really was proud of you, Justin, and she did understand your commitments in Chicago. Probably because she was just as committed to her patients as you are to yours, which makes you a lot like her."

"I'd have to go a long way to be like my grandmother," he said. "But I appreciate the compliment."

"Like I said, we could hold back on some of the changes."

He shook his head. "No, I want this place turned into a real medical clinic, and the sooner the better."

"What about the herbs?" she asked. "Because you know Eula's regulars won't necessarily come just because you renovate her house if you don't treat them with the kind of medicine they've always known."

"I know they won't trust my medicine because they want swamp medicine." He chuckled. "And they won't trust a white clinic either, Mellette. It might look good, but I did spend a lot of years here, living with these people, and I'm pretty sure a glaring white medical clinic in the middle of Big Swamp won't fit in."

"See, you do have a feel for the people here after all."

"I *was* the people here for a while. Which is one of the big problems."

"Maybe not as much as you think. And you could be one of the people here again, if you wanted to."

He shook his head. "It's not me. I want to go home."

"This isn't home?"

"This is my sentimental home, I suppose. But it's not my real home."

"You *are* planning on staying around for the renovations, aren't you?"

"Actually, I need to go home tomorrow."

"So you expect me to do everything?" she

asked. “Because that’s not part of the plan. At least, not part of *my* plan.”

“The problem is, I have to speak at a medical symposium in a couple of days. I was asked over a year ago, and I can’t beg out of it at this late date.” And he wouldn’t have begged even if he could have. He needed to separate himself from this place for a little while, from the memories and the feelings that just wouldn’t let go.

“But you’ll come back when the symposium ends, right?”

That wasn’t part of the plan, either. But he knew he needed to come back to help Mellette, and he was fighting himself on that. What he’d originally envisioned was dropping in maybe six weeks from now to evaluate the progress, then maybe six or ten weeks after that for another evaluation. Then he’d hand the reins over to Mellette and get back to their former arrangement where he sent her a monthly check. It was easier that way. A monthly dip into the trust left to him by his parents, and he had a free and clear path for another thirty days.

But he was being tugged in a different direction, too. One that kept him here for those weeks, and kept him more available to Mellette, helping her with some of the burden, since what he intended to do was, essentially, to drop it all in her lap.

Which made him feel like a real creep for even thinking such a thing. “Come with me. Come to my seminar and spend a couple of days off in Chicago with me,” he said, more to keep him on the right path than anything else. Because once he got home, got caught up on the whirlwind… No, he needed Mellette there with him to pull him back.

“Seriously? Just drop everything here and go to Chicago with you?”

“Seriously, yes.”

“I…I…don’t know what to say. I don’t live a spontaneous life. Especially now, with Leonie.”

“You know your dad will love to watch her.”

“Chicago,” she said, as a smile slid across her face. “There’s this lovely restaurant—seafood—out on the pier.”

"And we can take a charter boat to see the city at after dark."

"Gosh, that sounds so tempting, but…"

"But what?"

"What about the clinic here?"

"Eula took her days off, and you deserve yours."

She thought about it for a moment, then with the exuberance of a child said, "I'll do it!" and threw her arms around his neck. "I'll really do it!" Then, realizing the position she was in, she backed away and blushed. "Sorry about that," she said.

"About what?"

"My exuberance."

"I'm not. I like spontaneous." But he'd liked the hug even more.

"I'll be fine, Daddy," Mellette said on her cell phone as she struggled her way through the masses of fellow travelers congregating in the corridors of Chicago's O'Hare International Airport, pulling her overnight bag behind her, trying to keep up with Justin, who was plow-ing through the crowds purposefully. "Just give Leonie an extra hug for me tonight and tell her I'll bring her a nice surprise when I come home." Something to assuage the guilt of spending the night away from her daughter.

"You just have yourself a good time, and don't worry about a thing here," Charles responded.

"I intend to have fun." What she hadn't told him was that half her reason for this trip was to make sure she got Justin back to New Orleans. Something had told her he might not have come back. At least, not in the near future. And being there with him was her assurance he would.

Mellette pulled her overnighter through the whooshing pneumatic doors on the lower level just outside the baggage claim area, and headed to the line that was forming at the curb, where at least fifteen people were ahead of her, all awaiting cabs and different destinations. It was an orderly process, with taxis lined up and approaching their pick-ups one by one. "This is crazy," she commented to Justin, as someone bumped her practically into his arms.

"Which is part of the reason I love it here," he said, laughing as he steadied her.

"It would drive me crazy having to deal with this many people all the time. I mean, I can't even begin to imagine the emergency rooms…."

"You get used to it."

"Not me," she said. "Definitely not me." She stepped up to the curb as the next taxi in line arrived to pick them up. It was old, fairly grungy looking, but it would take them away from the madness of the airport and that was all she wanted. "But you really like this?"

"I love it. Love the variety, the action, the people."

"We are different, aren't we?" A difference that, as far as she could tell, would never be narrowed. Well, Justin was entitled to his lifestyle, just as she was entitled to hers. Only his was going to have to wait a little while longer.

Justin gestured her back into the inner sanctum, and she was only too glad to follow him through the hall back to his office, which turned out to be just about the nicest office she'd ever seen in her life, and that included all those places she'd seen in architectural magazines, showing famous doctors' even more famous offices.

"This is it," he said, motioning for her to sit. But not at his desk. He showed her to a sitting area where cushy leather chairs and couches were arranged in front of a huge plate-glass window that overlooked Lincoln Park and, beyond that, the expansive Lake Michigan—calm today, with its occasional whitecap lapping the shoreline. It was a stunning view, one that suited the stunning chrome-and-leather office and, for a moment, all Mellette could do was stand and stare at the stark contrast to everything at Big Swamp.

As much as she stared and admired, she wasn't envious. This wasn't her world. Wasn't even a world where she was comfortable. "This is—" she drew in a sharp breath, trying to gather her wits "—amazing." So different from what she'd imagined. Somehow she'd pictured him in something far less toned and trendy.

"The building over there..." He pointed to

a high-rise buff brick building that sat kitty-corner to his office and jutted up by a good thirty or forty stories, yet sat somewhat dwarfed by the steel-and-glass buildings surrounding, almost engulfing it. “That’s where I live. Top floor, penthouse. Just a quick walk to work. No alligators to contend with.”

“You’ve come a long way since Big Swamp,” she said. “Did Eula ever see any of this?”

“Once. It made her…nervous. She said it was too much. She didn’t like being up so high. It made her feel vulnerable.”

It made *her* feel vulnerable, as well. “But it is too much, Justin. I mean, I’m on sensory overload right now.” She turned to face him, was stunned by how much of a doctor he looked. Was stunned even more than she hadn’t seen that until now. But in her defense, back in Big Swamp all she’d seen had been jeans and T-shirts and disheveled hair, which looked good on him. Yet here he was in a perfectly starched white lab coat, and it made him seem like more of a doctor than she’d counted on. And that looked good on him, too. Justin Bergeron was equally gorgeous in both his worlds. "It does have its appeal, I must admit."

"So you understand why I have to come back?"

"If that's what your heart dictates, then, yes, I understand. But I need you in Big Swamp for a while, Justin, even if your heart isn't there. And you've got to know that's part of the reason I accepted your invitation…to make sure you did come back with me."

He chuckled. "We're not so different, you and I. A large part of my reason for inviting you was to make sure you would drag me back. I knew that once I was back in my world I might not be so inclined to leave it again for a while."

"It's not a simple thing, trying to get the clinic up and going, and at the same time trying to keep the medical practice there running." *And be a mother,* she thought. "I've got patients to treat, and carpenters and electricians to deal with." She shook her head. "All that plus right now I'm spending more hours there than I ever worked before, which wasn't part of the deal. This arrangement was to allow me more time with Leonie, not less, and while I agree to all this in the short term, I won't do it alone. Not even for a week or two. I just can't. I can't do it alone."

"I know that," he said, stepping up dangerously close behind her at the window. "And I'm only saying I might have stayed here, not that I definitely would have. But bringing you here was just my—"

"Insurance," she cut in.

"That, plus I really did want to show you my life, the things I love, what I have going here. And you work so damned hard I thought a couple days off would do you some good.

"So give me about an hour here, then we'll go see a little of Chicago. It's going to be a beautiful night to go down to the pier, ride the Ferris wheel, have dinner, take a boat ride."

"I need to check into a hotel and get ready."

"My condo has a guest room, so I'd just assumed…"

"That I'd stay with you?"

"It's better than a hotel. No bedbugs. None of

those who-knows-what kinds of stains they find with black lights in hotels. No one boiling unmentionables in the coffeepot."

She laughed. "You're ruining hotels for me forever."

"So you're not going to argue about staying at my place?"

"I'm not going to argue, but I also may never forgive you." She gave an overexaggerated shudder. "And, please, don't ruin anything else for me, like restaurants and public parks."

"Wouldn't think of it." He was chuckling as he showed her to a seat then exited his office. "Oh, and if you want anything to eat or drink—coffee, tea—just ask the receptionist. And the office has internet access if you want to work or talk to your dad back home." With that he was gone, leaving her there all alone in Justin's world—all alone to take in a different side of him. He was a minimalist, for sure. And very modern in his surroundings. Also very tidy. And, oh, goodness, he was clean. Even though he hadn't been in his office for weeks, there wasn't a speck of dust to be found anywhere, and she didn't need a pair of white gloves to prove that.

No wonder Justin didn't want to stay in the bayou. It must be driving him crazy, being around so much chaos. For heaven's sake, on some days there might be a lazy alligator or two in the yard. It didn't take Mellette five minutes to understand a completely different Justin than the one she'd come to know, who was living in a world where everything around him was pure pandemonium. He must have been going crazy there. If ever there was a case where worlds collided, this was it.

And as it turned out, his condo was pretty much like his office. Sparse of what she considered comfort. The bare minimum in furnishings, and all ultramodern. "I'd like to say it's lovely," she commented as they entered the living room, "but there's not enough here to really call it much of anything."

"I'm a man of few needs. Like to keep my life simple, which means keeping my surroundings simple. And just so you'll know, Eula hated it, too. Said it was too impersonal and cold."

"But if you like it..."

"I don't necessary like it or dislike it. It's just easy for me to keep myself organized if I don't have much to organize. Oh, and your room is the one on the left. Dress warm. It can get a little breezy out on the water, even at this time of the year."

The Ferris-wheel ride was lovely, and she couldn't remember the last time she'd actually been on one. Normally she was wary of heights, but at dusk, overlooking the pier as well as the city skyline, for a few minutes she felt like a little girl again, almost wanted cotton candy.

"This is amazing," she said as she huddled up in the seat next to Justin and gladly allowed him to put his arm around her for warmth, even though he'd bought her a souvenir hoodie with the words *Navy Pier* on it. His arm just made her feel safe, protected, and she liked that, especially when they swirled around the top of the wheel and for just that moment they were on the top of the world. "I haven't been on one of these since I was a little girl."

On the next trip to the top he pointed out his office, and on the trip after that his condo. Then all too soon it was over, and Mellette was almost as disappointed as the child in the car in front of them who cried when she was taken off by her parents. "That was almost worth the trip to Chicago."

"And the evening has barely started." For the next hour they strolled around the various shops along the pier, went through the stained glass museum and walked as lovers might, hand in hand at times, at others his arm around her waist. There were people everywhere, and concessionaires, and the whole length of the dock was lined with tour boats, people waiting for an evening excursion just to see the magnificent skyline.

"I could be happy just buying some toasted almonds and sitting here, watching the people," she said.

"Except we have dinner reservations in ten minutes, and a boat ride of our own after that."

"You didn't have to do all this for me, Justin."

He smiled. "Yes, I did. I mean, you're enjoying yourself, aren't you?"

"Loveliest night I've had in years."

"Then I had to do this for you." He took hold of her hand and pulled her in through a door and up some steps to a seafood restaurant. Sparkling grape juice was served tableside as if it was the most expensive wine in the world, and the lobster was divine. She'd been raised on crayfish and lobsterlike critters, but eating the real thing for her first time, dipping it with her fingers into the warm drawn butter… It was so decadent, so good, she didn't want the experience to end. But after they'd shared a generous slice of cheesecake it was over.

"So I know those crawdads you eat are mighty tasty, and I love them myself, but how do they compare to lobster?"

"Two different worlds," she said, as he slid his arm around her waist. "Crawdads, crayfish or whatever you want to call them, fit my world. Lobster fits yours. I don't think you can draw a comparison because there really isn't one. But I must admit I'm enjoying my visit to your world."

"Yet we're not so different. Different worlds maybe, but I have lived in both, and I understand yours."

"Understanding it and living in it are two different things. Admittedly, I'd hoped you would stay and run the clinic. Now I understand why you can't. This is where you belong."

Was it, though? He was beginning to question that, thanks to Mellette. He had to admit he liked being in a world where she was, and this would never be her world. "I belong there, too," he whispered. "Just not so much anymore. And I think my grandmother understood that when she came to visit me. Up to that point she'd really pressed me to come home, but when she saw my life here…I think I disappointed her. Or maybe the way I fit here disappointed her."

"You never disappointed her, Justin. I think she wanted you back again, but she understood."

As they reached the boat, the captain greeted then and showed them aboard. It was small compared to some of the other massive tourist ships, but sweet and smart, with an enclosed deck as well as an exterior one. “Make yourself at home,” the captain said. “We’ll leave port in about ten minutes and in the meantime help yourself to the array of desserts and fruits in the cabin. And as the doctor requested, sparkling grape juice. No alcohol.”

“Why do I get the feeling that we’re the only passengers?” she asked Justin as they stepped into the cabin and she saw a lush array of finger food.

“Because we are. The captain is one of my patients and he was only too happy to rent the entire boat out to me for the evening.”

“Well, I must say it’s much nicer than my boat.”

Justin laughed as he helped Mellette out of her hoodie. “Your boat’s a step up from a raft.”

“It gets me to work and keeps me safe from gators. That’s all I need. But I could get used to something like this taking me to work every day." She picked up a chocolate-covered strawberry and nibbled off the end as the boat lurched away from the dock. As it lurched, she lurched, too, right into Justin's arms.

"Takes a while to get your sea legs," he said, laughing, as she pushed away from his chest and noticed the strawberry stain she'd left on his shirt.

"I'm so sorry," she said. "Maybe if I could find some club soda we could get that stain out before it sets in."

"Don't worry about it. I've probably got fifty more shirts. Losing one for a good cause is no big deal."

"What's the good cause, Justin?" she asked, as they pulled out of harbor and the lights of the city began to take on a life of their own. "I know you're not trying to seduce me, so is this whole thing just a ploy to make me understand why you're not going back with me? Let me see your life and how much better it is here than in Big Swamp so I'll understand why my trip back home will be alone?"

"Whoa!" he said. "Where's that coming from?"

"It's coming from someone who's watching you try too hard to show me how good your life here is."

"Seriously, that's what you think this is about?"

"What else should I think?"

"That I'm trying to give you the best two days off you've ever spent. You don't take time off, and you don't spend time just doing something because it's fun for you. You're a great nurse, and even better mother, but where in your life do you leave time for you?"

She turned to look out at the old lighthouse in the harbor, liking the feel of the breeze on her face. It was at that moment she slipped off her wedding ring and tucked it into her pocket to save for Leonie. Moving on… It was time. Just a quiet, private little gesture meant only for herself. "It's not the way I planned my life, but it's what I got, and I'm doing the best I can to make the most of it. If it was just me, things would be different. But I have Leonie, and being a parent… That changes everything."

"Maybe it does, but don't you still have the right to hold on to something for you?"

"Right now, holding on to my sanity is enough." She chuckled. "There are days when I'm not sure I can do it, so at the end of my day, if I'm still sane, then I know it's been a good day."

"But what about you? What do you want?"

"A life where I didn't have to struggle so much, where I could spend more time with Leonie. Where I didn't have to make the choices I make just to stay practical. Once upon a time I used to be spontaneous. Maybe not to this extent, but Landry and I would do things…like take off for a day or two, no destination in mind, and just drive until we found the place we wanted to stay. And picnics…I loved picnics, where I could just lay back and see images in the clouds." She sighed. "That's a side of me you don't know, because I can't afford to let it out. Even this…one night, and I feel so…so guilty because I know I should be back home, working on plans for the clinic or reading a bedtime story to Leonie."

"But you're enjoying it."

"More than you can know, Justin. More than you can know."

"And you trust that there are no ulterior motives?"

"Let's just say that I half trust, and leave it at that."

He laughed. "I accept it because it's so…you. Mellette Chaisson, always on her guard."

"You have to be when somebody charters a boat for an evening sweep around Chicago." With that, she picked up a piece of pineapple and popped it into her mouth. "And tries to ply you with sparkling grape juice."

"Then you like?"

"I love," she said, turning to give him a kiss on the cheek. "Thank you for being so extravagant. I think I like this side of you."

"Well, for what it's worth, I am going back to Big Swamp with you, Mellette."

"Thank you," she said, quite simply. "For everything."

For the next hour as they cruised the harbor and, with his hand around her waist most of the time, and her head on his shoulder, to any onlooker they would have seemed like lovers. They certainly did to the captain and crew. And while the kiss Mellette gave Justin before they left the boat was circumspect, just a brief touch to his lips, the captain was already counting on the money he was going to make the next time Justin chartered his boat for this lady. And there would be another time. The captain was sure of it.

CHAPTER FIVE

THE TRIP, HOWEVER short, had been wonderful. But the symposium was now over and they were on their way back to Louisiana. A fact that made Mellette a little sad. Another day would have been nice. Two days was more than enough to be away from Leonie, but one more day in a different world would have been nice. "Thank you," she said as she relaxed back into the plane seat, awaiting take-off.

Their hands brushed across the seat console and neither one of them made an attempt to move. It was like touching him, even so slightly, meant their brief holiday had not ended.

"My pleasure. I was glad of the company."

"Even though it was my company?"

"Especially because it was your company. I live in one of the most amazing cities in the world, and yet I never take time to experience it. So for that I should be the one thanking you."

She smiled. "Your grandmother was always so worried about you because you never took time to relax. She said you drove yourself into the ground, working."

"It's the only way to get ahead."

"If that's all your life is about. Personally, I prefer having other things around me besides my job. I have my family, and I love doing things with Leonie."

"Which suits you, and I'm glad for that. But what suits me is what you saw. I work. Period."

"Will that ever change?"

"You mean, if I meet the right person, will she change that desire in me? Honestly, I don't know because I'm not looking. If it happens, then we'll see. But I could end up with someone just like me…"

"And you'd both live the very same life doing the very same things."

"Weren't you and Landry alike?"

"Not at all. He was a…I suppose the best way

to describe him was a dreamer. He had these grand ideas. So many things he wanted to try. I was the one who kept us grounded, but that was okay because it worked for us. We were…good. And the whole thing with Landry was you never knew which direction he was going. He made life a surprise, fun and spontaneous."

"And I thought you didn't like spontaneity."

"I do. Just not alone."

"I can see why you miss him."

"The worst pain has mellowed, and I can think back and even talk with fondness now about the good things we had. For so long I couldn't because it made me sad, made me cry. But I got past all that because I needed to hold on to the good times so I could share them with Leonie. I realized that all she was ever going to know about her daddy was what I would tell her, and if it came with tears…" She shrugged. "That's not the kind of impression I want her to have of him."

"So why are you doing this for my grandmother?"

"Doing what?"

"You know, trying to wrangle me out of my guilt issues. I mean, I understand the whole part about your clinic involvement and how it's your ticket to a better future. But what's in it for you to make good on your promise to my grandmother?"

"Who says there was a promise?"

"I do. You're working much too hard on me for there not to have been."

"She knew you would feel guilty about not being there, and she asked me to help you through it. That's all."

"And even though you didn't know me, you agreed to do it?"

"It made her feel better. And I owed your grandmother so much. She helped me through my crisis after Landry died, was so very kind to me, taught me how to get back out there on my own again, and one little promise was the least I could do for her."

"So that promise was what?"

"Just to help you get through it. That's all, really. I made a simple promise to someone I loved, and I want to honor that promise."

"She thought I'd feel guilty?"

"She knew you would. And, truthfully, I wasn't in favor of the way she wanted to handle her last days, but it wasn't my decision to make."

"I'm glad you respected her wishes enough to honor them, but still—" he shrugged "—it hurts."

"I know, and I'm sorry for that. I really am. But I didn't know you then, and I did owe so much to your grandmother. I'm sorry, Justin. For both you and your grandmother. And I did try to talk her out of her decision. She just wouldn't be talked out of it, though."

She refused the drink from the flight attendant; Justin took a cola. And neither of them said another word for several minutes. Mellette simply sat there with her eyes closed while Justin thumbed through the dog-eared catalog selling expensive gadgetry. So it went until the flight attendant bent over Mellette a little while later and asked, "When you booked, you booked under the name Dr. Justin Bergeron. Would you be a medical doctor, by any chance?"

Mellette's eyes snapped open.

"Yes," Justin said, instantly alarmed. "General surgeon."

"Then would you mind coming with me, Doctor? There's someone I'd like you to see."

Without another word, Justin unfastened his seat belt and followed the flight attendant forward, leaving Mellette alone to wonder who might be sick, especially as because they were sitting in first class, there wasn't much more ahead of them but the pilot's cabin.

"How long have you been short of breath?" Justin asked the pilot, who was still strapped into his seat, sweating profusely and gasping for breath, while the copilot was busy assuming charge, alternately looking at his controls and glancing across at his colleague.

"About ten minutes," the man choked out.

His color had evolved to a pasty white, Justin noticed. "Are you nauseated? Light-headed?"

Justin wedged himself into the cabin as best he could, while the flight attendant, a stately middle-aged woman named Lana, stood behind him, blocking entry to the cabin. “Chest pain?” Justin asked, as he took hold of his wrist to check the pulse.

“Some nausea, not much. Thought I’d eaten something that didn’t agree with me. Not pain in my chest either so much as tightness.” He indicated his sternum, straight down the middle.

“Shoulder, arm or jaw pain?”

“Some, in my jaw.”

Justin turned to Lana. “I need an aspirin.” Then he asked the pilot, “Do you have any history of heart disease? Or are you on any kind of medication?”

“No medicine except an occasional ibuprofen when I get a headache. Haven’t had one in weeks. And I passed my physical last month with flying colors,” the gray-haired man said. “Is this a heart attack, Doc?”

“Might be,” Justin said, taking the aspirin and popping it into the pilot’s mouth. Then he turned to Lana. "I put my medical bag in the overhead storage. Would you get it?"

A couple of minutes later Justin backed away from the pilot's seat, having diagnosed a thready, rapid heartbeat and low blood pressure. "Go and get my flying companion," he instructed the attendant, as the pilot let out a groan, indicating that he was getting worse.

The copilot, who'd been doing his level best to concentrate on flying the plane, turned to Justin just as the pilot, Jack Foster, reached up, clutched his chest and fell into unconsciousness. "Do I need to make an emergency diversion?" he asked.

"The sooner we get down, the better," Justin said as he laid his fingers on the pilot's neck. "I'd like to get him to a hospital as fast as we can."

Without another word to Justin, the copilot was on his radio to find an alternate airport where they could make an emergency landing.

"Justin?" Mellette said, wedging herself into the tiny cabin. She took one look at the situation and nodded. "Has he had an aspirin?"

"Just a minute ago. BP's low, pulse thready,

difficulty breathing, tightening in his chest, jaw pain…" He grimaced. "Classical symptoms."

Her natural reaction was to glance toward the copilot's seat, to make sure the plane was being flown. Once she was satisfied they were safe, that the young man taking over looked not only competent but calm, she took a step closer, then lowered her voice. "I'm going to see what kinds of emergency supplies they have on board the plane. Be right back."

Outside the door, the flight attendant pointed to a cabinet where first aid and medical supplies were kept.

"What do we have available?" Mellette asked. She was primed to spring into action. Emergencies were her territory and it was difficult simply standing around, waiting to be oriented, when she needed to be working.

"A first-aid kit, portable oxygen bottles, an AED, automated external defibrillator and an EMK emergency medical kit, with various supplies and drugs."

"Such as?"

"A stethoscope, blood-pressure cuff, bag mask resuscitator, three different sizes of oral airways, nitroglycerin, aspirin, albuterol, injectable dextrose, 1:1000 epinephrine, oral antihistamines, IV antihistamines and cardiac resuscitation drugs, including IV 1:10,000 epinephrine, atropine and lidocaine. We've also got five hundred milliliters of normal saline, an IV drip set and a variety of needles and syringes."

Mellette couldn't help but be impressed by the flight attendant's knowledge. It wasn't quelling her need to move faster, but she was relieved that the airline was well equipped.

"And if Captain Foster needs to lie down, I'll get the gallery area cleared out and recruit a couple of men to help lift him there, where you and the doctor can work on him if you have to. But let me warn you that the entire plane's going to go into a panic once they know the pilot is incapacitated. We'll make the announcement and let them know that we have a second, equally competent pilot on board, but be prepared for some panic attacks and anxiety-related conditions to pop up, because I'm betting that's going to happen."

"I can imagine," Mellette said, glad of the warning. "By the way, does the AED have an ECG screen to monitor the cardiac rhythm?"

"It does, but it's a paddles-view only."

Which meant only one type of tracing out of twelve could be viewed, but that was much better than nothing. "Let me talk to Justin—Dr. Bergeron—and see how he wants to proceed."

Mellette stepped back in the cabin, where the pilot looked even more pasty than before. And he was certainly fighting for breath harder than he had only a minute before. "We've got what we need to maintain him, I think, but there's going to be more room outside the cabin, on the gallery floor, so the flight attendant's going to get that cleared for us. Oh, and she's expecting panic attacks from the passengers. Thought you'd want to know what we're going to be up against."

"One thing at a time," Justin said, as Mellette stepped back out to the galley to get the various drugs and set-ups ready for the pilot.

Almost as he spoke, two men appeared at the cabin door, ready to lift the captain to the area just outside the door. It was a bit of a struggle, getting him out of his seat in a space clearly not intended to fit as many people as were crammed in there. So to give them more maneuvering room, Mellette stepped back, essentially to the first row of first class, and stood in the aisle.

"What the hell's going on?" one impatient man snapped at her.

"Medical emergency, sir. And everything's under control."

"Is it the pilot?" he demanded.

"As soon as things are straightened out, someone will let you know," she answered, trying to sound as calm as she possibly could. Passengers were now straining to hear what she was saying, and she could already feel waves of panic coming from a number of them.

"I paid good money for my ticket, and I demand to know now!" he shouted in return.

"In due course," she said quietly as the men up front began to move the captain out of the cabin. As that was happening, Mellette deliberately stepped forward to just opposite the front lavatory door, hoping her presence there would block the closest passengers from seeing exactly what was going on.

"Due course isn't good enough!" the man yelled, unsnapping his seat belt and lunging forward. He grabbed Mellette's arm in an attempt to move her aside, but after years of wrestling rambunctious patients in the E.R., she packed a few good defensive moves and deftly slid out of his grip, managing to grab hold of his arm and spin him around so his face was pressed tight to the lavatory door.

"We don't need any more problems right now," she whispered to the man, "so I would suggest you return to your seat and buckle yourself in, or you'll be facing a security guard the instant you step off this plane."

A bold threat, and she didn't know if that was what would actually happen. But the last thing she needed while they were getting the pilot settled into position was some bull of a man rushing forward, causing problems.

"Better sit down," the old woman with the knitting magazine said. "I heard her talking to that man of hers, and she's not a person I'd care to tangle with."

Mellette turned to smile at the old woman, who gave Mellette a mischievous wink.

"Take your hands off me," the man demanded, but his voice didn't hold nearly the same threat it had earlier.

"Fine, but if you move one inch in the direction of the galley, I'll drop you to your knees next time."

Those words brought about a round of applause and cheers from the passengers in the front section of the plane. Two men seated in the first few rows of coach class stepped forward, each one taking an arm of the belligerent man to show him back to his seat. Or, in this case, shove him back.

"That was pretty good," the flight attendant whispered as she stepped back to allow Mellette into the galley area once the pilot was flat on the floor.

"All in a day's work," Mellette said, immediately slipping an oxygen mask over the pilot's face, then she set about the task of inserting an IV while Justin got him hooked up to the heart monitor.

"Guess I should be glad you didn't manhandle me that way to get me on board," Justin said, as the lines of the pilot's heart rhythm started flowing across the tiny screen. "But I suppose I'd better keep it in mind for future run-ins with you, shouldn't I?"

"I have defensive skills and I know how to use them," she replied, smiling over at him.

Out in the cabin, you could have heard a pin drop. It was as if all the passengers were holding their collective breaths. All behaving very well, including the combatant man, who was a bit red in the face, either from agitation or embarrassment. Mellette made a mental note to check his blood pressure after the captain was stabilized, just to make sure his outburst hadn't caused him any physical problems.

"Ladies and gentlemen," the copilot announced over the loudspeaker, "as some of you are witnessing, our pilot has had a medical emergency and is currently being treated at the front of the cabin. Please do not interfere with the process, please do not leave your seats and come forward, because we need all the space we have to stay unobstructed. And rest assured that I am a fully qualified pilot with ten years' experience, and the plane is functioning exactly as it should, with no difficulties. But you do need to know that we are going to be diverting our flight..."

"I've got the IV in," Mellette told Justin as the pilot continued to go over the plan, "so our choices of drugs are atropine and lidocaine." Without waiting for his response, she readied the lidocaine.

"You're good at this," Justin commented.

"I'm an E.R. nurse, remember?" she said as she swabbed the IV port and injected the drug.

"Then you're probably better at this than I

am, since I rarely get involved in emergency procedure."

She looked at him and smiled. "Probably."

He chuckled. "And modest, too."

"In the meantime," the copilot was wrapping up, "please sit back and relax. This plane is in no jeopardy."

"Unless the copilot has a heart attack, too," the belligerent man piped up, and was immediately shushed by the passenger behind him. The initial rush of panic subsided.

Back at the front, Mellette, who was kneeling over the pilot, took a look at the heart tracing and breathed a sigh of relief—not that any bad heart tracing was a relief, but she did recognize it indicated a blockage. And as far as they went, this one wasn't too bad. "I think today's going to be his lucky day," she said, finally settling back into a more comfortable position for the duration of the ride. "If you can call a heart attack lucky. Because I don't think this one's going to turn out to be too serious."

"And he did have one semiskilled doctor and

one highly qualified nurse on board," Justin added as he palpated another blood pressure, then sighed in relief when he saw that the numbers were stabilizing.

"Don't be so hard on yourself. I'm sure if he'd needed his gallbladder removed, you'd have been Johnny-on-the-spot." She laughed. "But you were good. Especially in such cramped quarters."

Justin looked around, as if he'd only just noticed how cramped they were. "Did I ever tell you that I'm claustrophobic?"

"Seriously?" she asked.

He nodded as he fought to control his own breathing, which was beginning to turn a bit shallow now that he wasn't preoccupied by the emergency.

"Need oxygen?"

Justin shook his head, drew in a ragged breath. "Need wide-open spaces."

She glanced down at their patient, who was doing nicely, then across at Justin who was not. She adjusted the pilot's oxygen mask, then took hold of Justin's hand. Held it for twenty seconds, then let go when she felt the spark that passed between then. A real electrical jolt, it seemed, even though she knew it couldn't possibly be. "Sorry, Doctor, but that's all the bedside manner you get from me."

"You've got better things to do than give aid and comfort to a hopeless claustrophobic?"

"Actually, yes, I do." She grabbed the blood-pressure cuff, then stood and headed back to the cabin, on the verge of her own little panic attack as she marched straight over to the man who'd given her quite a struggle. He was still red in the face. Too red, considering the time that had passed since the incident, and her fingers automatically went to his pulse. But he jerked his wrist away from her.

"Don't touch me," he hissed.

She could hear wheezing coming from him.

"I think you might be having a medical crisis, and I just wanted to check you."

"You touch me, and I'll sue you! I'm warning you, lady…" He sucked in a lungful of air, and the wheezes became more apparent.

"Are you asthmatic? Do you have a history of blood-pressure problems or any other diagnosed condition?" she persisted.

His answer was to glare at her and, if anything, turn even more red.

"Are you having difficulty breathing, or chest pains?"

He still didn't answer.

"Feeling anything peculiar that you don't normally feel?"

"Would that include my anger toward you?" he snarled.

She knew it was an irrational reaction, knew his agitation was escalating by the second, yet she couldn't force her medical attention on him. So she shrugged and started to walk away. But two steps into her departure she turned back to him. "You've got something going on, and I don't know what it is. I need to examine you to be able to help you, but if you're going to sit there being so pig-headedly stupid, then go ahead and have a stroke or a heart attack or whatever it is you're going to have. Just keep in mind that you've forbidden me to help you, which means you can, and probably will, die if that happens. I have a planeload of witnesses who heard you."

Not that she wouldn't help the man, even against his orders if it came down to it. But she was hoping a little scare tactic might get him to cooperate. She didn't need another emergency on this plane.

"Nice bedside manner," Justin said as she bent down next to him, preparing to sit back down and help monitor the pilot.

"You do what you have to do. In this case, some arm-twisting."

"Remind me not to get on your bad side."

"What makes you think you're on my good side?" she asked, arching her eyebrows.

"Well, for starters, you haven't injured me. Haven't even threatened to injure me."

Mellette laughed at that. "Give me time. I'm sure you'll earn it somewhere down the line."

"I'm sure I will," Justin said, shifting his position, going from kneeling to sitting cross-legged with his back to a storage pantry.

"You doing okay on the claustrophobia?"

"Not really. The galley has shrunk by half in the past five minutes."

"Want me to see if someone on board has some alprazolam or diazepam? I'll bet if I put out the call, a lot of people will have it."

"I'm fine," he said, wiping a bead of sweat off his face.

Instinctively, Mellette reached into the medical kit, pulled out a square of gauze and handed it to him for a wipe. "I'm afraid of heights," she admitted.

"Like in an airplane?"

"No, because it's enclosed. But climbing trees, and standing on the side of a mountain, looking down. When we were young, my parents took us on a mountain vacation—rented a cabin, had a very nice week planned. But I wouldn't get out of the car and walk to the cabin door because we were sitting on the edge of a bluff. I wanted to, even tried to. But I couldn't get out of the car to save my soul."

"How old were you?"

"Seven or eight, I think. And the thing is, we already knew I had a hard time with heights. Even going upstairs to my bedroom at my parents' is a challenge, because if I look down I get dizzy, and if I get dizzy I start hyperventilating."

"So I take it you and Leonie live in a one-story?"

"Blessedly close to the ground. The thing is, I've learned to control it because I know it's just an irrational fear popping out. Heights won't hurt me—" she smiled "—unless I fall from one. Which won't happen because I don't take the risks that will put me up very high." Except the Ferris-wheel ride they'd taken. But that hadn't been a risk as she'd been in his arms the whole time.

"So did you spend your entire vacation in the car?"

She shook her head. "After a couple of hours my dad asked me if I trusted him. Of course, I said yes. Then he promised me nothing there would hurt me, and he took me by my hand and led me inside. Once I was in the cabin I was fine, but going back and forth outside, where I could see how high up we were…that's what didn't work so well. But Daddy always held my hand, and after that we took our vacations at the beach."

"Well, just between you and me, my greatest fear is getting trapped in a stalled elevator with a bunch of people. If that ever happens to me, I'll be the one in the corner, on the floor, going fetal."

She gave him a fake frown. "I don't think fetal would be a good look for you." She looked up as the flight attendant approached. "The pilot has cleared us for an emergency landing, so we'll be setting down in about ten minutes. Oh, and the gentleman in the first row would like to see you," she said to Mellette. "He thinks he might be experiencing some difficulty."

Mellette pushed up off the floor, grabbed the emergency kit and smiled. "My adoring public waits."

"Don't twist his arm so hard it breaks," Justin teased. "Because I don't do bones."

Back in the cabin, Mellette took the seat next

to the man, whose name turned out to be William, and immediately put the blood-pressure cuff on him. He didn't look at her. In fact, he kept his head back against the headrest, with his eyes closed.

"It's too high," she told him, once she'd taken the reading. "Have you ever been diagnosed with hypertension?"

He shook his head.

"Well, the good news is your pulse is fine, and the wheezes I heard earlier have diminished. I think you might have been having an anxiety attack, but I am concerned about your blood pressure because it's dangerously close to stroke territory, so I'm going to have an ambulance waiting for you once we get off the plane and send you to the hospital to be looked at."

He rolled his head to look at her, and opened his eyes. "If this turns out to be nothing, I'm going to sue you for delaying me," he said.

"I'm sure you will," Mellette said, settling back into her seat and fastening in for the landing.

Her patient merely rolled his head back to look

forward and closed his eyes again. And twenty minutes later, as they strapped him to an aisle chair and took him out after the pilot had been escorted to an ambulance, he looked at Mellette. "I want you to give me your name and address and a copy of your credentials," he snapped. "Immediately!"

Mellette merely laughed as she bent down to him and whispered, "Don't hold your breath."

"Maybe you should have broken his wrist," Justin said as he pulled her overnight bag down from the overhead locker.

"As miserable as he is, I don't think he would have noticed."

They were the first two to be let off the plane, and they followed their respective patients to the medics waiting to take them to the ambulances. Then, as was customary, they were asked to report to the airline office and give details of the event. Consequently, they missed the connecting flight that would have gotten them to New Orleans in a relatively respectable amount of time.

"And I supposed you're going to blame me for the flight delay in case we don't make it to New Orleans by tonight," Justin said as the two of them were finally free to go.

"It crossed my mind," she said, holding back a smile.

It was going to be five more hours before she and Justin and would get back to New Orleans, and by the time that new arrival time had sunk in, Mellette was too exhausted to put one foot in front of the other. She'd already spent half an hour talking to Leonie on the phone, and another hour browsing all the Lambert–St. Louis International Airport gift shops for gifts to take back to her daughter. Then she'd bought a romance novel to read. All while Justin stretched out casually on the seats and snoozed.

So typical, she thought to herself, remembering back to Landry and how easy it had been for him to fall asleep anywhere, any time. While she, on the other hand, had had a hard time going to sleep in their own bed, let alone anywhere else.

But Justin did look kind of cute sleeping, she had to admit, with his mouth half-open and his hair all mussed. He really was a handsome man. More classically handsome than Landry, who'd been a rough-and-tumble outdoors boy. He was larger than Landry, too. More muscled. Taller by a couple of inches.

Landry, she thought as she settled into a seat next to where Justin was sleeping and rubbed the empty spot on her ring finger. He'd been everything she'd ever wanted. Her perfect companion. As she slid down into her seat and shut her eyes, she counted on his image popping into her mind to comfort her, the way it always did. But tonight it didn't.

Nothing was there except the frightening void of empty, black space, which caused Mellette to sit bolt upright, blink herself back into the moment and fight off the panic rising so fast it felt like her heart was going to explode. Landry… For that instant he'd been gone from her completely, leaving her with the sense that he was never coming back. She'd forgotten what he'd looked like. How could that happen? How could his image just vanish like that?

Mellette wanted to close her eyes again to see if he would comc back. But she was too frightened, and her pulse hadn't settled down enough.

"You okay?" Justin asked groggily, as he sat back up.

"Just fighting fatigue. No big deal."

He sighed and scooted over to her, until they were touching, then he put his arm around her shoulder and pulled her even closer. "You fight too much," he said. "It'll wear you out."

"I have a lot of things in my life to fight," she said, giving in to the comfort he was offering. It was a man's touch she hadn't expected to like, or even to accept. And it surprised her how easily, and how willingly, she allowed herself to practically melt into his arms. But that was exactly what she was doing and she was enjoying it more than she should have. Any other time she would have recoiled, jumped up, moved to the other side of the aisle. Right now, though, she was just too tired and, admittedly, she did like the feel of having him there with her. Liked it more than she should have, maybe even more than she'd let herself admit to.

Liked it so much she let her eyes close. And didn't sit bolt upright when she still couldn't find Landry in the darkness. As the only one she needed there was Justin.

CHAPTER SIX

IT WAS HARD, facing the changes—the changes going on inside himself to do with Mellette, after holding her for those hours in the airport while she slept. He was attracted to her. More than attracted. In fact, he wondered if she might be the one to turn his world upside down. But leaving Chicago and coming back here? Could he do it? And if he did, could he be happy? Somewhere logic needed to meet emotion, and he wasn't sure where that would happen, or how.

Also, it was hard, facing the changes going on with his grandmother's house. He hadn't realized how attached he'd been to it, or to the memories. Too much was changing…changing too fast. All of it was his doing, though. The medical clinic and what he was feeling toward Mellette.

Admittedly, his new feelings for her were what had him the most confused, because they weren't the normal physical fluff he experienced when he spent time with a pretty woman. She was substance. It just engulfed her like a cocoon. So while that probably should have scared him—and he'd have been smart to have been scared—it didn't. It was more like it intrigued him, made him want more…more of her.

He'd been too long without a woman, he tried to tell himself. And while that was true, the other thing he had to admit was that he'd never had a woman like Mellette in his life. So maybe she wasn't really in his life so much as close to it, but she was close enough that it was making him think. Confusing thoughts. Conflicting thoughts.

"Better color?" Mellette asked, stepping up behind him.

"Much." Rather than going with white paint for the house's exterior, which she'd originally planned, Mellette had chosen a charcoal gray, which was as near to the original color as it could get. But she'd added trim colors that the house had never had before—lighter gray around the windows and a rich brick red for the chimney, door and flower boxes under the windows, which made the place look welcoming. "It's…different. Going to take some getting used to. But I like it."

"Changes aren't always easy, are they?" she asked him, giving his arm a sympathetic squeeze then looping her arm through his and pulling him toward the house. "Even when we expect them and want them."

"Even when they're for the best." The welcome sign was conspicuously missing and it surprised him how much that single, small subtraction affected him. But it did, and it caused a hard lump to form in his throat, probably because it had always been his habit to look up at the sign looming over the door every time he walked in. But times were changing, weren't they? And this was her project, not his. So he had no reason to complain. At this late date, he had no legitimate call to remind her of his suggestions, either. No reason to say put back the sign because, damn it, he missed it!

"Did you save the welcome sign?" Justin asked Mellette, on the off chance she'd tucked it away somewhere, as he stepped up on the front porch and saw that the old wicker furniture, too worn to be functional, had been replaced by new. He was glad she'd left his grandmother's original porch swing, though. "The one that used to hang over the front door?"

"Yes, it's in a safe place and ready to hang back up once the project is completed."

"Good," he said, having this sudden urge to sit down on Eula's old swing and just…swing.

"Want me to hang it now?"

He shook his head. "No, that's not necessary. Just as long as it's hung up at some point." He was surprised how sentimental he was about something so meaningless, but he was. That sign signified…home.

"Well, if you change your mind…" she said, then went chasing off after a man in a hard hat who had a stack of lumber over his shoulder.

That was when Justin went inside, took two steps in the door and was surprised to see the progress that had been made. Nothing inside resembled what had been here before…not even in the very rough stages, as this was. Walls were gone, studs and wiring exposed. The old wooden floor had been torn out, replaced by boards over which new flooring would go. Even the old windows were missing. "Damn," he muttered, impressed as hell and sad at the same time.

"You like it?" Mellette asked, stepping in just behind him.

"It's not what I expected."

"You wanted a clinic that looked like a clinic, and that's what you're paying me to give you. So…would you like the grand tour?"

He wasn't sure he was ready for it. But when he turned to look at Mellette, he wasn't sure he'd ever seen anyone as stunningly beautiful in all his life. And it was her excitement over the transformation that was making her so pretty. It shone in her eyes, in the way she smiled, in the way she concentrated on every little aspect of every detail in the front room. With her Creole mixed coloring and a slight scarlet flush of excitement rising to her cheeks, she was a real breath-taker. Someone who, under different circumstances…

No! He didn't have a right to those thoughts. There were too many obstacles, the first being the fact that she still considered herself a married woman. Her bond to that union was so strong, even now, that she wasn't going to let another man in. And even if she did, it wouldn't be him because he wasn't leaving Chicago and she wasn't leaving here. So what was the point of even thinking out the what-ifs of this situation?

Still, he couldn't help but admire beauty when he saw it. In Mellette he saw it in ways he'd never seen it before. And that included her take-charge attitude. The more he was around it, the more her strong character was growing on him and all he could think of was the missed opportunity back in Chicago. She'd kissed him as a friendly gesture, but what if he'd returned that kiss with some passion, rather than just standing there like a dope and not responding? "Sure, a grand tour would be good," he said, mentally kicking himself.

Of course, one kiss didn't change the outcome of their destinities, did it?

"Well, this is the new reception area, and I've had it enlarged so we can turn it into a proper waiting area. I think a lot of folks will still prefer to sit outside and wait on Eula's porch, the way they always have, which is why I've added new chairs. Oh, and the window boxes. I know she wasn't into frilly things, but with the new paint I just thought that the exterior needed some dressing up, and Eula did love the flowers in her garden, so I took the liberty of planting some of them in the new window boxes.

"Even though we're turning this into a more functional clinic, I still want it to have some homey touches, which is why, when this waiting room is done, it's not going to be so…traditional."

"Should I ask what you mean by that?"

She shrugged. "It's going to be about simplicity. A place to pour yourself a good cup of chicory coffee. A checkerboard to play a quick game while you're passing time. A couple of rocking chairs. And a nice sound system for some zydeco."

"Zydeco," he repeated. Music popular in the bayou.

"Of course zydeco! What other kind of music would you expect?"

Of course zydeco. It made sense, actually. In fact, all Mellette's choices so far had made sense. "I made a good choice."

"Zydeco was my choice," she said defensively.

"But you were my choice. And you have no idea how you glow when you're working. It's very attractive on you."

"Oh," she said, as the scarlet in her cheeks flushed a little redder. "I'm not a big one for flattery," she said. "Most people flatter because they want something in return, and all you're getting is what you're paying me to do."

"Which precludes me from paying a compliment when that's what's due?"

"You picked me out of a registry. I was a name to you when you chose me, so it's not like you really chose me so much as you chose my credentials for the job."

"Like I asked before, does that preclude me from paying you a compliment when it's due?"

"And like I said, I'm not a big one for flattery. You're paying me to do a job and I'm doing it. Purely business, Justin."

"Whoever said it wasn't?"

"Flattery leads to other things."

Like sleeping together, entwined in each other's arms in the airport. And enjoying it. "It's not my intention to lead to other things, Mellette, and I'm sorry if my compliment made you feel uncomfortable."

She blushed even harder. "It was a year after my husband died. I wasn't ready to date, had no intention of getting involved. But there was this doctor at the hospital—a man I worked with occasionally. I thought he was a nice man, someone who was just trying to be kind to me. And he flattered me, Justin. All the time. Said things that didn't mean much at first, and eventually the flattery…it ramped up. Became very suggestive. I asked him to stop, told him I wasn't comfortable. But he didn't, so I went to my department head, who took it from there.

"Then this doctor had the audacity to tell my supervisor that I'd been asking for it, that I'd been the one who was suggestive, and if it weren't for the fact that my mother was chief of staff, he'd have filed a complaint against me for sexual harassment. Me, harassing him! I mean, I know I was vulnerable right then, maybe not picking up on the clues, but...but I wouldn't have done that. Wouldn't have even let him go on for so long if I'd really taken a good look at what he was doing. I was still so numb, though."

"Your supervisor didn't believe him, did she?"

Mellette shook her head. "Not for a minute. But word got out, people talked. I got shunned. You know how it is. Anyway, after that, I just don't trust people's motives unless they're pretty straightforward. And while you've been pretty straightforward..."

"I make you nervous."

"Flattery makes me nervous because you never know where it's going to go."

His heart did go out to Mellette, being so assertive on one hand and so unsure of herself on the other. To have loved someone the way she'd loved Landry… He couldn't even imagine that. "Where does complimenting you on a job well done fall in your list of things I shouldn't do?" he asked.

"See, that's well within my bounds, because it's professional. Just telling me that I look good while I'm doing the job isn't."

"Then instruct me when I get it wrong, because I do want to know, Mellette. I want you to be comfortable working here." And especially comfortable working with him.

"I will. Speaking of which, let's go to the first exam room, formerly the forward downstairs bedroom. It's had quite a transformation." Sighing, maybe a breath of relief, Mellette gestured for Justin to follow her down the hall, past a new space that was little more than the size of a large closet. "Doctor's office," she said. "I was going to have it up front in the parlor, but decided to use that as my own office space since I don't expect the doctor will be here all that often. And I need something different than the kitchen."

It was apparent she was nervous, the way she was wringing her hands, so he took particular care to stay well away from her—walked to the window on the other side of the room while she remained standing in the doorway. "When you say the doctor, I'm assuming you mean your dad?"

"My dad, maybe others if I can recruit some volunteers form New Hope. Oh, and let me warn you, the next time you see my mother, she's not going to be very cordial to you. She absolutely hates the fact that my dad has agreed to come back to work, even for a few hours a week. And you're the one who's going to feel the bite of her wrath, I'm afraid. I mean, she's not happy with me giving up my job at the hospital to come and work here full time, and you're going to get the backlash from that, as well. But when Daddy told her he'd be coming out here occasionally..."

"In other words, you've just put me in direct

opposition to arguably the most powerful doctor in this part of the state."

"Something like that." Her eyes finally crinkled into a relaxed laugh.

"And she wants to kill me."

"More or less."

"Then it's a good thing I'll be back in Chicago when the project wraps up."

"Trust me, Chicago's not far enough away to escape my mother's anger."

"But doesn't she see that this clinic is a good thing?" Justin asked, as he surveyed walls now torn down to the studs.

"I think she sees that bringing our kind of medicine to the people out here is good, but not at the expense of her family. And the thing about my mother is she's still very…Creole. She's one of the most highly regarded physicians in the country, yet she still has respect for the herbal aspects of bayou medicine."

"So she's not in favor of modernizing the clinic?"

"She's in favor, but not to the point that the old

traditions here will be lost. She loved your grandmother, by the way."

"She knew her?"

"Not knew. But she did meet her once. Came here when I first took the job to see what kind of place I was working in, and she and Eula sat on the front porch and talked for hours. They talked as doctors, and talked as women who shared similar backgrounds, and my mother truly respected her for the work she did here in Big Swamp."

"But she's not in favor of getting you or your dad involved."

"She likes having her family close, and this isn't close enough to suit her. I think she believes she can't protect us well enough while she's in the city but we're out here, which is like a strange and distant land to her."

"You're just like that, aren't you? About Leonie. Your whole life is built around protecting the people you love, and especially your daughter." He sneaked a casual glance at her as she looked away because he liked the way her face lit up, but he wasn't fast enough to avert his gaze as she turned back and caught him.

"What?" she asked.

"I like the way you come alive when you talk about the things you love. It's nice to see you relax that way."

"I—um—um—" she stammered, looking for a comeback. But when she didn't find one she dived back into her protective shell. "To be compared to Zenobia Doucet… That's maybe the nicest thing anybody could ever say about me." She paused, then gestured for him to follow her upstairs, where she intended to show him that modernization and not transformation was taking place. Just new paint, new windows, new varnish on the wooden floor. Nothing else to change the bedrooms. "You meant it as a compliment, didn't you? Comparing me to my mother?"

"Only if you don't think I'm trying to garner a favor by paying the compliment." Running his fingers over the formerly green, now light yellow walls, he looked outside to the yard, to his old escape route, and smiled fondly. "That was my old escape route. One I used so many times when I was a kid, and it was such a simple way to get away for a while.

"Out the window, down the tree, hide behind the clump of sweet azaleas to make sure the creaking caused by opening the window didn't awaken my grandmother, then, when I was sure I was in the clear, make my way along the fern bed to the hickory tree. After that, run like hell across the open expanse down to the old boathouse. Once past that I was home free!

"Then it was either grab my bike and take off on one of the back roads, or untie the canoe and paddle myself out of there, maybe meet up with Johnny Redbone and Bobby Simoneaux, go into Grandmaison and hang outside the door to Guidry's Inn and hope some of the beer bottles getting tossed in the can out the back door still had beer in them.

"Or go down the road to old man Lazier's place and sneak in the back of his barn to grab a few leaves of that weed he was always drying behind his regular tobacco. Sometimes we got lucky and found a jar of his moonshine in the rafters, one he'd overlooked when he'd taken the others into his house. Those were good nights for a bunch of fourteen-year-old boys."

Good nights, good times, he thought. Rough times, too, that had earned him his bad boy reputation, and certainly now he'd never do those things he'd done back then. But he looked back on the old days with fondness, because he hadn't had such a bad childhood. He had been a bad child, though. One set down in the middle of what could have been a very good childhood if he'd let it happen. Which he hadn't. Even so, he'd turned out pretty good in spite of it.

"So whatever happened to your coconspirators?" she asked.

"John Redbone's now a judge on the bench over in Baton Rouge, and Robert Simoneaux is a high school history teacher. No thanks to me and the way I'd led them. And make no mistake—I was the ringleader."

"Sounds like good times for a young boy."

"Restless times. I was always restless."

"But like your friends, you found your place, and the restlessness stopped."

Except that he was feeling restless again.

"Your grandmother always knew where you were going. Did you know that?

"She told you?"

Mellette nodded. "When you thought you were sneaking out, she was sitting up, worrying. And she didn't like what you were doing one bit, but every time she tried to discipline you, you threatened to run away. She was afraid you would. So you'd sneak out the window, and she'd stay up all night waiting for you to come back, praying you'd be safe."

"Damn," he muttered. "Why didn't she ever tell me?"

"You left home when you were, what? Sixteen?"

He nodded. "Just a week shy of turning seventeen. And I was getting into all kinds of trouble by then, and she…she wanted me to fix the messes I was making for myself. Wanted me to take responsibility…" He turned to face her. "I guess I'm not really surprised that she knew. Maybe the only thing she didn't know was how to handle a smart-ass kid who wouldn't be handled."

"Her only hope was trying to teach you to be *smart*. At least, that's what she told me."

Maybe one of the reasons he didn't want to be here was that he didn't want to see, through adult eyes, the kind of pain he'd caused his grandmother. It was a bitter pill to swallow. But it was a pill he deserved. "What about the second bedroom downstairs...my grandmother's sewing room? Is it going to be turned into an exam room, as well?" he asked, deliberately trying to change the subject. Talking about the many ways he'd hurt his grandmother was still too painful.

"Identical to the first exam room."

"And the kitchen?"

"I haven't been able to make any changes there. The kitchen is where Eula most loved to be, whether it was cooking a meal for herself or friends, or fixing one of her herbal concoctions. So when I think of Eula, I picture her in the kitchen, and I just haven't had the heart to change any of it."

Funny, but when he pictured his grandmother, that was where he thought of her, too. There in the kitchen, or sitting on her front porch. "Maybe you won't have to," he said, hoping that was the way it would turn out.

"So what do you think so far?"

"I think it will work. It's going to take some getting used to, but since you're keeping some of the more homey touches, as well as keeping some of the house intact, I think people will generally respond positively."

She shook her head. "Nobody's even coming here right now. If they do, they won't come inside…prefer the porch. They think what we're doing here is disrespecting Eula's memory, and they want no part of it. So I'm either working on the front porch treating patients, or making house calls."

"House calls? Seriously?"

"Three or four a day right now. And trust me, no one out here wants the kind of medicine they think you're trying to cram down their throats. They literally peek out the windows to make sure you're not with me when I visit them."

"So I'm getting the blame for the way they're acting?"

Mellette smiled. "You sure don't think I'm going to take the blame for any of this, do you? I've got to work with the people, so I'm doing everything I can to stay on their good side. And since they need an enemy..." She tapped the air with her index finger, pointing at him. "It's all yours, Doctor, and you're welcome to it."

"Good thing I've got broad shoulders."

"Good thing," she agreed as she stepped backward into the hall. "Look, I need to go and see Paul LeCompte. He's not been feeling too well—gastric upset, and I want to take him some tea."

"Tea?" Justin questioned.

"Your grandmother's special recipe for Paul. Got to look it up and put it together for him."

"Ah, yes, her patient filing system, as she used to call it." He was referring to her volumes of old, dog-eared, spiral-bound notebooks in which she'd kept the precise instructions for the herbal remedies she used on each and every one of her patients. One book for each letter of the alphabet, except the *X-Y-Z* volume, which was combined.

Justin walked into the kitchen, opened an old-fashioned Hoosier cabinet that had seen well more than a century of use—the cabinet where she'd kept her herbs—pulled out the *L* volume and turned to the Paul LeCompte page. Not to be confused with the thirty or so other LeComptes in her book. "It says chamomile tea, with one pinch cinnamon, one pinch cayenne, two juniper berries smashed and three pinches of ginger."

"Eula was pretty precise about her prescriptions."

"One pinch, Mellette. That's the kind of medicine you're practicing? A pinch of this, two smashed berries..."

"If it works it works."

"Then why has Paul LeCompte been coming here for a quarter of a century with the same complaint?"

"See, here's the thing, Justin. Your grandmother certainly had the ability to cure certain things. She was always very humble about calling it cured. She always called it treated. But as you well know, there are things that require lifelong treatment, chronic problems like Paul LeCompte experiences that will never be cured."

"The man eats too much greasy food. Always has. Cut out the grease, cut out the stomachaches and who knows what else his diet is doing to him."

"Are you going to be the one to tell him that? Because you know how the people are around here."

"I'll tag along, if you don't mind."

"And do what? Irritate him?"

"My presence here irritates just about everybody else, so there's no reason he should be the exception."

Mellette quickly assembled all the LeCompte tea components, put them in a small paper bag, then dropped it into her traditional medical bag and headed for the back door, which meant they were taking Eula's old pickup truck for this house call.

"I'll drive," Justin said, grabbing the keys off the hook by the back door and rushing ahead to open Mellette's door for her. It wasn't so much to be gentlemanly, since he wasn't sure how she'd take the simple gesture of courtesy. But the passenger's door had been stuck for more than twenty years, and it took some effort to persuade it to open. Like a couple of kicks, a few swear words and another kick.

"Some things never change," he said when the door finally popped open. He helped Mellette in, then shut the door and smiled. Yep. Some things never changed. And in a way, he was glad about that.

Paul LeCompte's cabin was fairly isolated in the woods, and if not for the mailbox on the dirt road, his weedy, overgrown driveway would have been easily missed. It was a pretty area, really, full of cypress trees and huge oaks, with a never-ending maze of brackish waterways separating his little piece of land from that which sat adjacent to his, and coincidentally was owned by his brother Robert.

The moss hanging down from every tree resembled a silverish-gray beard adorning the many branches, quite eerie to lay eyes on for the first time. It was still used as ticking in mattresses by a lot of the folks who lived in the bayou. Justin knew for a fact that his grandmother had occasionally used it to treat what she called sugar, and what he called diabetes.

"It's about time you got yourself back where you belong, Justin," Paul LeCompte said, pronouncing Justin's name *juice-tan,* the way most of the people in the bayou did. "Didn't think you'd ever have the guts to show your face around here again, not after the way you treated poor Eula, God rest her soul. Not being here for her last days..."

Mellette looked over at Justin to gauge his reaction, saw his jaw clench, saw him ball his hands into fists. Laid a reassuring hand over his left fist and was quite surprised how well he kept his cool.

"She was a mighty good woman," Paul continued. He was seated in a rocker on the front porch of his blue clapboard house, swatting at mosquitoes and snapping pole beans he'd picked from his garden. "Deserved a whole lot better than what you ever gave her, all that nonsense before you ran away."

Mellette stepped up behind Justin and took hold of his right arm. Could feel his biceps tense up. "Justin's just here to help me, Paul. He's very good with treating gastric upsets such as yours."

Paul's response was to snort. "Give me Eula's tea. That fixes me right up, and it's all I need." He looked up at Justin, who'd yet to speak. "And I don't want the kind of medicine you'd be having me take."

"I didn't come here to give you medicine, Paul. If you want to keep on having the same stomach pains you've been having for as long as I can remember, that's your business."

"You're right, young man. That's my business."

"But if you'd ever care to see just what the diet of yours is doing to you—to your heart and arteries, and to your blood—I'd be glad to prescribe the blood tests you'd need."

"I'm just fine," Paul said although, admittedly, he did look a little stressed. "Don't have anything wrong with all those things you mentioned."

"And you're, what? About fifty now? Bet you've never had a full physical, have you?"

"Don't need one," Paul snapped. Then he looked at Mellette. "And no offense to the lady, but even if I did get that physical, I wouldn't be having it from a woman. Just doesn't seem right."

"Well, I'll be here for a few days. And I'd be glad to accept a bowl of those pole beans in exchange for a physical," Justin offered.

"Don't you go holding your breath, young man. I've done just fine up to now without having a doctor interfering with me, and I'll do just fine in the future."

"Well, if you feel any tightness in your chest, or lightheadedness, or experience any shortness of breath…you know where to find me."

"Only if I'm looking for you, Justin, which I won't be."

"Pain in your arm or shoulder, trouble *going,* back spasms…"

"What was that about?" Mellette asked as they walked away from Paul LeCompte's cabin.

"Well, when I opened my grandmother's notebook to his page, I saw she'd written the description of a hypochondriac, so I decided to play to that a little."

"A little? It was a masterful performance, Doctor." She applauded him.

"And if it worked, he'll be coming around shortly for me to have a look at him."

"It has to be you, since he's not about to let me take a look." She laughed. "That's pretty sneaky, Justin." She pronounced his name the way Paul had.

"It's a good way to mix medicines."

"But that's only one person."

"One is a start," he said, as he kicked the truck door until it opened. "I think you need better transportation out here."

"The truck works fine. Starts up every time and gets me where I need to go. People trust me when they see me in it, but if I were to show up in something shiny and new, I can't even imagine how they'd react."

"For a rich girl, you're pretty down to earth."

"See, that's the thing. My family has wealth, but I don't. If I did, I'd quit my job and be a full-time mother."

"Is that your dream?" He shut the truck door and went around to climb in the passenger's side, then looked back at the house and saw Paul standing there, watching him.

"For now. I love my work. But I'd love to spend more time with Leonie, maybe even take a couple of years off and stay with her until she goes to school." It wasn't going to happen, of course. But it was a nice dream.

"Look, can you give me a couple of minutes? I think Paul is trying to work up the courage to tell me something, and I'm thinking maybe I should go back up there and talk to him."

"And let him take you to task the way he did before?"

Justin shrugged. "I've got broad shoulders."

"Then go, talk. I'm sure what he has to say isn't meant to be heard by a woman, anyway."

Which turned out to be the case, as far as Paul was concerned. "What you said about having trouble going," he said to Justin. "I can go all right, but sometimes it's a little…slow, if you know what I mean."

"I do know," Justin said, feeling quite pleased that someone was actually seeking out his medical advice. "And there are a lot of ways to take care of that."

"Ways Eula would have used?" the man asked him. "Not that I would have mentioned such a delicate matter to her. But are you talking about treating me the way she would have approved of?"

His grandmother had been a formidable woman, even after her passing, and it pleased him to see how much the people here were still loyal to her. "Depends on what I find when I give you a physical. But there are certain remedies of hers that might help you. The best I can promise you until I've had a look is that I'll be open-minded."

The man snorted. "We'll see about that, Justin. We'll just see."

"So are you going to get a bowl of fresh pole beans?" Mellette asked him.

"Seems so, some time tomorrow, most likely." Justin climbed into the truck and started the engine. "And he'd appreciate it if you weren't anywhere near him when I have to do that physical. Which, by the way, means I've got to get some walls up in one of the exam rooms today."

"They're not scheduled for another week."

"Are the materials there?"

"If you mean the Sheetrock, yes, it's there. But can you put it up?"

"I worked in construction for a while when I was saving up to go to college. So yes, I know how to swing a hammer."

"I'm impressed," she said. "Landry worked for his family in construction. In management, though, not in the field. They wanted him to be more involved in the business end of the company, but he loved the actual hard physical work. Said it made him a good kind of tired at the end of the day."

"I know how that feels. I had a chance to go into hospital administration, but I couldn't imagine not being involved in patient care. It's what I love, and, like Landry, I like that good kind of tired I feel at the end of the day, the kind of tired that lets you know you've done something useful."

"Well, I could ask Tom if he can get someone to help you with the walls."

Justin shook his head. "If I can get Amos Picou to come over and steady the sheetrock when I put it up, I'll be fine."

"And you'll have an exam room all ready for Paul LeCompte by tomorrow?"

"You've never had his pole beans, have you? They're worth the effort."

As they made their way back across the bumpy road, Mellette twisted ever so slightly in her seat in order to catch glimpses of Justin out of the corner of her eye. Certainly, she didn't want to out-and-out stare at him, but she did enjoy watching him. Probably because he surprised her. Just when he proved he was one thing, he changed, almost magically, before her eyes. Yesterday she hadn't been sure he'd actually return with her and today he'd just convinced Paul LeCompte to come in and surrender to a prostate exam. And now he was going to hang Sheetrock.

Justin was a man of many moods and faces, she decided. Had she'd seen them all, or were there more to come? In a way, she was anxious to find out.

"I have a good recipe for fixing pole beans," she said. "Maybe since my mother won't be home tomorrow night, we could invite Daddy out and have him bring Leonie, maybe invite Amos Picou, and have dinner? I'll cook, of course. Get us some ham shanks, potatoes and onions, maybe shrimp? And we'd need cornmeal for corn bread."

"You cook?"

"Some. After all, I *was* married." *Was* married, not *am* married. It sounded strange saying that, because she still told people she was married in the present tense, not the past. This was the first time she'd ever referred to it in the past and it was odd. Not odd in a horrible way, though. Odd, as in the way it was supposed to be. Life was progressing. Moving on.

"Sounds like a meal fit for a tired doctor, which is what I'm going to be by the time dinner rolls around tomorrow night."

"We don't have to do it," she said, suddenly feeling very unsure of herself. It wasn't like she was asking him on a date or anything like that. But this was her first real step away from Landry, and while she'd expected to feel guilty, she didn't so much. That was probably even more of a surprise than her arranging this impromptu little dinner party, which was a pretty big surprise in itself since she didn't usually have time to socialize.

So what was it about Justin that was causing her to step away from all her caution? Maybe, just maybe she liked the man. Or maybe it even went beyond that a little. Was she ready for that, though? Falling in love again? Could it be time? Was she able to move on and give herself totally and completely to another man without Landry coming between them?

These were things she needed to consider in private—far, far away from Justin's charm and influence. Because to love Justin and to have him love her back meant a compromise that scared her. It might mean moving away from here and starting over in Chicago, of all places.

She didn't know if she could, didn't know if she was ready for that drastic change. But it came with Justin, and there was no reshaping that. So she had to proceed carefully. Very carefully.

"No backing out now. I haven't had homemade corn bread in years, and you don't know how much I'm looking forward to it. But let me warn you beforehand that if the food is good, I intend to be lavish with flattery. Just want you to be prepared for that."

Mellette laughed halfheartedly. "Don't you worry about the food. It'll be good."

"Just like everything else you do," he said, then hurried to add, "Statement of fact, not flattery."

Mellette laughed again, this time a genuine laugh, and for the first time realized that she'd laughed more with Justin than she'd laughed since Landry's death. It was good being carefree again, not always having the weight of the world on her shoulders.

Impulsively, before she jumped out, she leaned over and kissed him lightly.

"Wh…?" he began.

But she held her hand up to silence him. "Don't ask, because I don't know. Don't have a clue, and I don't want your opinion."

"Well, I'm not objecting," he said, snaking his hand around her neck. "In fact, if I may be so bold as to reciprocate…" The second kiss was longer, deeper. And when Mellette pulled back from it her lips felt swollen.

"We shouldn't be doing this," she said, trying to reclaim some composure.

"You're probably right."

"I am?"

He nodded gravely. "It's unnatural. Two people attracted to each other wanting to kiss. It throws off the whole balance of things."

Mellette laughed. "You don't know how close you are to the truth."

"You're not ready? I mean, I totally understand if that's the case."

"I think it's the opposite, Justin. But I need time to figure it out. We don't exactly have a smooth road in front of us however we proceed, do we?"

"You ever heard of living for the moment?"

"You ever heard of planning ahead?" She leaned over and this time kissed him on the cheek. "I need time," she said wistfully, hating the word, hating the concept. But it was true. She did need time. And a clearer head than she had at this moment. "Now, I've got some herbal concoctions to mix, then some computer filing to do, and you've got, well, whatever it is you need to be doing."

"Buzzkill," he complained, feigning a hurt look.

Mellette laughed as she headed back into the clinic. Truth was, she hoped he discarded his shirt and got on with his carpentry. If only he knew the thrill that gave her. If only…

CHAPTER SEVEN

GUILTY PLEASURES. Okay, that was what she'd call this and she'd try hard not to feel guilty or disloyal. But she was human after all, and female on top of that. Which was why sitting in the front room, sipping lemonade and watching Justin swing a hammer, had such appeal. He was shirtless, sweaty, his jeans were riding dangerously low, and all of it together was a lethal combination. In fact, if the other Doucet sisters were here, she could just imagine them lined up together, drinking lemonade and watching the show with her.

And what a show it was. Justin was the picture of vital health and strength, everything a man should be. More so, the graceful way he slung that hammer…and the way he kissed…

Watching him gave her chills and caused beads of perspiration to break out on her forehead at the same time. Watching from afar, of course. Only from afar. And with the utmost discretion, since she would not allow herself more than a few stolen peeks from time to time as she went about the task of starting to computerize patient files—a tedious, dry task she wasn't too happy to be doing.

That was why she was allowing herself those occasional peeks at him, she kept telling herself. They were a distraction from the mundane task; something to help her refocus on what she needed to be doing.

She had to admit she enjoyed what Justin was so generously putting on display, and the only thing that might have made it better was if he'd had a leather tool belt riding even lower on his hips than his jeans.

Landry had looked good in a pair of jeans, too. Intellectually, she remembered that he had, but the image wasn't quite there any longer, and she gasped when she realized just how much she was enjoying Justin's exhibition. She felt disloyal and felt a horrible, knotting sensation begin in her stomach. She suddenly thought she was going to throw up.

Jumping up from her desk, Mellette ran to the bathroom, slammed the door shut and simply leaned against it, almost hyperventilating. What was happening to her? Why was she being so faithless to Landry? Sure, she'd taken off the ring. But the feelings wouldn't come off, and she still had these moments of panic when she wondered if she deserved to be happy again. Survivor's guilt was what they called it, even though she'd simply interpreted that to mean she was missing her husband.

She still missed him, but her heart was expanding, taking in someone else, and it scared her. Sometimes she was so sure she could move on, yet other times…

"You okay in there?" Justin called from outside the door.

"Fine," she said, her voice wobbly.

"You looked pale when you went charging down the hall. Are you sure you're okay?"

"Just a little too much heat and humidity out

here in Big Swamp," she lied. "I think we're going to need some kind of air-conditioning installed." Slowly, she let herself slide down the door, until she was sitting in a crumpled heap on the floor. "Let me splash some water on my face," she said as tears streaked down her cheeks. Mellette, normally the strong one, felt so weak, so confused. She didn't know what to do. "Don't…know… what…" she whispered as she sobbed quietly into her hands. Things were changing too fast. Spinning out of control. And she didn't know if she wanted them to. Or if she could make it stop now that it had started.

And it had definitely started.

"She's a mighty fine woman," Amos Picou said, as he steadied the Sheetrock against the studs while Justin nailed it in place. "You could do worse."

"I'm not doing anything," Justin said. "Mellette's still very much married to her husband."

"Who's been gone for nearly three years. I know Miss Mellette is having a hard time moving on, and I have sympathy for what she's going through, mixed emotions and all. But one of these days she's going to be standing straight again, and you need to have yourself ready if you want a shot at her. I'm telling you, boy, she's one mighty fine woman who's going to have her pick of suitors when she wants them."

"If by standing straight you mean ready for a new relationship, yes, I'm sure she will be. But I won't be here to see it." And that was a problem both he and Mellette recognized, or that kiss would have turned into more than a kiss. Of that, he was positive.

"Is that what you think? That you're not going to be around?"

"That's what I know. As soon as this clinic is done, I'll be gone. And Mellette can stand as straight as she wants, but I'll be standing back where I belong, on the shores of Lake Michigan." He spoke harshly, trying to cover up his own mixed emotions. "I've got to be going home, Amos. I don't have any other choice."

"She could be falling for you. Those are the

symptoms I think I'm seeing. Which makes that one of your choices, son. Maybe your biggest choice."

"And what makes you an expert?"

"Been in love. Know the look of it." He laughed from his belly. "Know it when I see it on two people, the way I'm seeing it on you two."

"You were in love?" Justin asked, somehow surprised to hear the confession. "Guess I never thought you were the type."

"Oh, I was the type, all right. Once when I was sixteen. Miss Xenia was my momma's friend. Beautiful woman in all the ways a woman should be beautiful. With some fine legs—merciful heaven, she had fine legs. Like Miss Mellette. Only problem was she was my momma's age, and my momma knew I was having these feelings. She threatened to hit me with a broom if I ever embarrassed myself around Miss Xenia."

"Did you ever get hit?"

"Oh, I got myself a good whamming one day. Was on my way to fetch some sugar for Momma, and had to pass right by Miss Xenia's house. 'It's hot out there today,' she said to me. 'Bet you'd like to come in for a nice, cool glass of lemonade.'"

"Did you?"

"You bet I did. I was in that door so fast my head was spinning."

"And?"

"And her lemonade sure was sweet. Best lemonade I ever did have."

"We're not talking lemonade in the literal sense, are we?" Justin said, chuckling.

"Let's just say that Miss Xenia made that awful transition from boy to man pretty damn good."

"But your momma found out?"

"After a while. And like she promised, she took the broom to me. But it didn't matter none, because my sweet drink of lemonade had up and moved away."

"And you never saw her again."

"Nope, and I'm glad I didn't. First love was sweet…real, real sweet. You can't go back, though, once it's over. The memories sure were good. Still are. But they didn't stop me from falling in love again."

"With my grandmother?"

Amos nodded. "That love was never returned, but I never treated it the way I should have, either. But I had me a real nice friendship that lasted a long, long time. It was enough."

"But was it, Amos?"

"Most of the time," he said sadly. "Not all of the time, though, because every morning, no matter what else was to come, I woke up alone. And you don't want that, boy. It feels like there's a big emptiness in you that's going to suck you in, and no matter what you do to fill it with other things, or try to forget it, it'll come back the next morning and you've got to deal with it all over again."

"If she didn't love you, why didn't you move on?"

"And go where? This swamp is what I chose. Got myself landed here after my other life didn't work out so well, knew this was where I belonged. Had me a fine life whittling trinkets to sell in town to the tourists and picking herbs and living close enough to Eula so that I didn't always feel so empty."

"Did she know how you felt?"

"I expect she did. And she respected it. But I never got the sense her feelings for me were the same. She was so wrapped up in taking care of the folks down here after your granddaddy left her, I don't think she had room for much else. Except you."

"Ah, yes. Me. The great disappointment."

"She understood human nature, boy. Knew your disappointments and frustrations. Knew you weren't adapting well from your grand life to being raised in Big Swamp. But she did the best she could."

"I know she did," Justin said solemnly. "And for what it's worth, I'm sorry she never returned the feelings you had for her."

"Me, too, boy. Spent a lot of years being sorry, and I've got some big regrets because I never tried hard enough. And with the way I've seen you looking at Miss Mellette, I think maybe you need to do some trying, too."

Justin took one powerful swing and hit the nail dead on, then took a couple more swings to drive it all the way in. "It can't work. Even if I could get past her husband, I'm going home and she's not about to leave here."

"You sure about that?" Amos asked, handing Justin another nail.

"I'm not sure about a thing. I mean, I'm attracted. I'm maybe falling in love. I've never seen a woman with so much strength and determination. She's a force, Amos. A real force. And I'm not sure I even know how to approach someone like her on an intimate level, let alone carry it through to wherever it might go."

"One step at a time, boy. You take yourself one step at a time."

"Not sure that's enough to get me past Landry."

"Oh, with the way Miss Mellette's been watching you for the past hour, I just have me this great big hunch that door is wide-open."

"Seriously?" Justin asked, moving back to take another swing.

"Seriously, boy. As they say, it's time to wake up and smell the coffee."

"It's been one hell of a day," Justin said, settling into his grandmother's porch swing. It was going on to midnight, and every muscle in his body was screaming.

"Starting out in Chicago and ending up here. Longest day of my life," he added, stretching, then yawning. "So why are you still here?"

"Got caught up in the work."

"It's not too late for you to go home."

She shook her head. "I respect Big Swamp, but I don't travel out here at night."

He laughed. "Some of my best times in Big Swamp happened at night. Always had a healthy respect for what's out here, but I don't think I was ever afraid of it."

"Poisonous snakes, alligators, bobcats..." She shook her head. "I'm a city girl, Justin. I might work in the bayou, but I won't put myself in danger here."

"Yet look at all the families growing up out here."

"That's their life. What they know. If I'd grown up here, I'm sure I'd have a whole different attitude or perspective. Or maybe I wouldn't. I mean, you grew up here, and you ran away when you were sixteen."

"Not because of the wildlife."

"From what I understand, you *were* the wildlife."

He chuckled. "I was restless. That's for sure."

"Why?" she asked. "Why were you so restless?"

He gazed at her in the dim yellow light, sitting in a wicker chair, legs tucked up under her. She was stunning. Absolutely stunning. And the thing was, he doubted she even knew how beautiful she was. Mellette prided herself on her competency, yet she was so unassuming when it came to her looks. They were certainly looks that could get under a man's skin.

"I've asked myself the same question a lot of times, and never really come up with an answer.

Maybe it's because I saw the bayou as limiting… for me. I think I always knew I wanted to be a doctor, but how can that happen when this is where you live?"

"You leave."

"Like I did."

"But you were on fire before you left, Justin. At war with the world."

"I *was* angry. But never with my grandmother."

"Did she know that?"

"I don't know. After I grew up, and got over the rage, I tried to make it up to her. Helped her every way I could."

"But that never felt like it was enough, did it?"

He shook his head. "It might have, though, if she'd accepted anything I offered. But aside from you, she rejected pretty much everything I tried to give her."

"Because you were giving on your terms, not hers. She had her life here, Justin, and she didn't want to leave it. Just like you don't want to leave your life in Chicago. She fought to hang on to what she had every bit as much as you're fighting to hang on to what you have. And in the end you get what you get, whatever that turns out to be. For Eula, it was being at odds with the person she loved most in the world. And for you… well, I don't know, as the last chapter hasn't been written yet."

"How did someone so young end up with all the wisdom in the world?" he asked.

She scooted out of her chair and headed for the door, stood there for a minute, waiting for Justin to get up and go inside with her. "Life dealt me a blow I didn't expect. I've had lots of time to do the retrospective on it."

"We've both had those blows, but you came through yours with so much grace."

"Because I had to be an example. It wasn't just about me."

"But I made my blows all about me, which makes me selfish, doesn't it?"

"Your grandmother lost a son, too. But she turned her personal tragedy into something that was all about you."

"Until she lost me," he said, swallowing hard. "I never saw it that way before."

She took hold of his hand. "She was the one who was full of grace, Justin. Not me. I was just coping the best way I knew how, and leaning pretty heavily on my family to get me through. I don't think you've ever leaned on anybody, have you?"

"No," he said. "I've always gotten by—"

"On your own," she interrupted. "And that's sad. Because life is meant to be shared, even the bad parts of it. I'm sorry you've never known that."

Suddenly, without warning, she stood on tiptoe and brushed a light kiss across his mouth. It wasn't a particularly provocative kiss, neither was it a sexy one, but it burned all the way through to his soul. And he was the one who felt his knees go weak. Wasn't it supposed to be the other way around?

"And that's where this discussion ends. So, on that note, I'm going upstairs and to bed," she said, as if nothing had happened when, in fact, everything had just happened. “I’ll be in Eula’s room. You can have your old room. ’Night, Justin. Sweet dreams.”

“Good night, Mellette,” he said, as the screen door banged shut. “Sweet dreams back at you.”

Sighing, he sat back down on the swing awhile longer, positive his shaking legs weren’t ready to carry him up the stairs yet, and listened to the night sounds. The calls of locusts and frogs, the rustle of the opossum. No, he’d never been afraid here. Not of the wildlife, anyway. But something else, something very real had just terrified him, and he had no idea what to do about it. Not a single clue. Because he could feel himself being pulled in a way he didn’t want to go. Or did he?

Could he live here again? Could he start a new life one more time? Could he finally come home?

“Didn’t snap ’em,” Paul LeCompte said grumpily as he shoved the basket of beans at Mellette when he walked through the front door the next morning. It was early, she hadn’t even had her coffee yet, and she had no idea where Justin was this morning. She'd heard him come up the stairs a good hour after she'd gone to bed, had tossed and turned and punched her pillow so many times it had a permanent knuckle indentation in it. What had she done? Why had she kissed him again when she'd promised herself she wouldn't do that?

The truth was, she didn't know. It had just happened. She'd felt like it. It had seemed the right thing to do at that moment. But it had come with a lot of regrets after the moment had passed because she knew where and how this thing ended.

So she'd tossed and turned, and listened to Justin thumping around in the room next to hers for a little while. And if that wasn't bad enough, she'd tried visualizing in her head what he was doing with each little thump and thud, which had kept his image vivid in her head. Then all had finally gone quiet, and she'd been left to her explosive and confusing thoughts, the ones that had kept her awake for a good hour after that. The ones where she'd promised herself she wouldn't go a step further with Justin, no matter what.

Nowhere in her jumbled head had she made room for the notion that Paul LeCompte would be waking her up just shy of 7:00 a.m. with a bowl full of pole beans.

"I…um…I'm not sure where Dr. Bergeron is," she said, feeling self-conscious in her nightie and bathrobe.

"Well, go and find him. I don't have all day to sit around here waiting for him to show his face. I came for that physical, and if he's not here to give it to me, I'm leaving and not coming back. And I don't like what you're doing to the place. What Miss Eula had here was fine. Just fine."

She wondered if Paul would even care that Justin had worked for hours building a private exam room for him. Sure, it was still in the rough, but walls were up and there was enough equipment in there to call it respectable. "Give me a minute," she said on her way to the kitchen to set down the beans.

"Sounds like my patient's in a bad mood,"

Justin said as she entered the kitchen through the back door. After she'd set the beans on the kitchen counter, he poured and handed her a cup of coffee. "I'm assuming you like it black and strong," he said. "It suits your personality. Only it's not chicory."

"I like chicory."

"I like coffee the way it was meant to be… from real coffee beans. Not chicory. No chicory added, either." Chicory was a Southern popular, earthy-tasting herb either substituted for or added to coffee.

She smiled as she clung to her coffee cup. "That's right. You're not a Southerner anymore, are you?"

"Oh, I'm Southern. Just don't have a taste for all things Southern, especially chicory. Even if it's supposed to be good for my liver, stomach and spleen."

"And your kidneys," she added. "Don't want to leave them out. Oh, and let me compliment you. You know a little more about herbal medicine than you let on."

"Eula raised me around it. What do you expect?"

"I expect that you should probably go and take a look at Paul LeCompte. I don't think he's going to wait very long to see you."

"I might need assistance."

"Do you really think that man's going to let me assist you, especially given the kind of exam you're doing?" Mellette shook her head. "Don't get me near that, Justin. I'm warning you, these people here are pretty set in their ways and that man out there is the worst of them. There's no way I'm going near him."

"Coward," he said, heading through the kitchen door.

"Darn straight I'm a coward," she called after him, then slid into a kitchen chair and tucked her legs up under her as she sipped her coffee, thinking about her promise to Eula to help Justin get through this. It had been her dying wish. What could she have done? "I'm working on him, Eula," she whispered. "He's not easy, but I'm doing the best I can." She was doing more than she'd ever expected.

The problem was, she didn't think her best was good enough. Justin was here because she'd done everything but tie him up to keep him here, but he didn't need to be kept here under duress. For Eula's last wish to work out, Justin had to want to be here. And for that he had to be happy again, at peace with himself.

"It wasn't a promise I should have made," she said, as she took another sip of coffee. No, it definitely wasn't a promise she should have made. But Eula Bergeron had been one persuasive lady, who'd found her tender heart and gone to work on it like an expert cardiac surgeon.

Sure, she'd been particularly vulnerable because of Landry's death, which had made her vulnerable about Eula's deteriorating condition. She'd made all kinds of promises to Landry in those last days, as she'd done to Eula. That was who she was. She couldn't help it, didn't have an excuse, either. The lady with the tough exterior and the take-charge demeanor had a very soft spot at her core, and there was nothing she could do to overcome it. She probably wouldn't even if she could.

Sighing, Mellette went back to the stove to refill her coffee cup, then took it upstairs with her while she got herself ready for the morning's work. She had three patients who'd actually made appointments, which meant she probably had nine more who hadn't. Then this afternoon she had four house calls. Plus somewhere in there she had a dinner to prepare, which, admittedly, excited her as much as anything had for a little while, probably because it was as close to a social life as she'd had in months. A dinner party, she thought as she stepped into the shower. Yes, she was looking forward to it.

"He agreed to take both medicines—Miss Eula's and mine," Justin said as Mellette stepped out of the bedroom into the hall, her hair still wet from her shower. She looked so sexy with wet hair and bare feet. Such a simple look—khaki shorts and a white T-shirt—and he was all but aroused. Fat lot of good that would do him.

"How'd you work that out?" she asked, toweling her short hair.

"Honest, man-to-man talk about the consequences of an enlarged prostate, and where a treatable condition could lead."

"Ah, yes. Go straight to the manhood and they always listen."

"Of course they always listen." He smiled as he averted his eyes, even though she was fully dressed. "Those kinds of things are near and dear to a man's heart."

"Even to Paul LeCompte's?"

"Especially to Paul LeCompte's. He's quite the ladies' man in these parts."

"Our Paul LeCompte, the one who snarls?"

"He did ask if you were seeing anyone," Justin replied with a grin.

"No…seriously, he didn't really do that, did he?"

"Cross my heart," Justin said, keeping a straight face and crossing his heart.

"I hope you told him I'm not looking."

"I told him you were…taken."

"Taken? By whom?"

"He didn't ask. But I think he assumed it was me."

"Why would you do that?"

"Are you interested in him, because I can tell him—"

She swatted at Justin. "Don't you dare. You've already said enough."

"You sure? Because he does like the ladies."

"I have patients to see, and if you're able to convince any of them that you're not the idiot they remember you being, then you can have part of the patient load." With that she marched into her bedroom, slammed shut the door so hard the Bergeron family pictures hanging on the blue-and-white-flowered wallpaper in the hall rattled. The one of Justin riding his new bike on his eighth birthday fell off the wall and the glass cracked.

Laughing, he picked it up, looked at the smiling face of the boy, and thought back to that day. Eula had saved her money and bought him a brand-new bike, not a used one like all his friends had. It had been red and shiny, and maybe for the first time since he'd gone to live with her he'd felt like he belonged there.

Up until that day he'd been so…lost. Orphaned so young and dropped into a lifestyle he'd known nothing about. He'd gone from well-off to poor. Living with a woman his mother had avoided because of their differences and whom his father had escaped because he'd wanted more than she'd had to offer. Nothing had worked, nothing had fit him.

Then that day, when Eula had given him the bike…the look on her face had said everything. She'd loved him, had made such a hard sacrifice to please him.

Everything had changed that day, and for a little while he'd stayed happy. But then he'd wanted a car. There had been no reason why he shouldn't have one, except that the money his parents had left him, and it had been a considerable amount, had been held in a trust. As an administrator,

Eula had refused to dip into it. "You want a car," she'd told him, "go find a job and earn it." It had been the same with nicer clothes, electronic games. Things other boys his age had had. "You want them, you go to work and buy them."

In the mind of a young teen, that hadn't been fair. That money was his. Rightfully his. And his grandmother had no right keeping it from him. So he'd lashed out. Said hurtful things, done hurtful things. Told her he understood why his dad had wanted to get away from there and why his mother had hated her. They had been harsh, ugly words. Yet through it all Eula had held firm in her resolve, for which he thanked God now, and would do every day of his life.

But he'd been so bad to her back then that it had become difficult to get past it. Sure, he'd tried making it up to her when he'd got older and had understood exactly what he'd done. Tried to get her to accept an apartment in New Orleans, somewhere where she could take life easy. Invited her to Chicago, as well. Or anyplace else she wanted to go. She had been content with her life the way it was, and he always wondered if that was the case or if he'd broken her heart so badly it couldn't heal. It had made it dreadfully difficult to face her for such a long, long time.

But that eighth birthday… He'd been happy then. Truly happy. "Too bad I can't go back to that feeling again," he whispered as he hung the photo, cracked glass and all, back on the wall.

Too bad Mellette couldn't go back to a happy time, either.

Too bad they couldn't go forward together and find that new happy place. He could almost picture them together. But there was nothing about them that would ever work out. Nothing at all.

CHAPTER EIGHT

IT WAS AN intimate little dinner party. Amos showed up early with fresh-caught shrimp, then Mellette's dad and Leonie arrived, bringing a delicious bread pudding he and Leonie had made together. And Paul LeCompte decided to come, too, since he'd provided the pole beans. There'd been no invitation extended and apparently no invitation was necessary, as he simply strode through the door and asked when supper was ready, then proceeded to sit down at the dinner table as if he was the guest of honor. In a way, he was, as Paul merely being there was a huge show of faith in Justin, otherwise he wouldn't have barged in and made himself at home.

So they ate sausage, chicken and crawdad jambalaya, with seasoned pole beans and corn bread, and talked lightly around the table, enjoyed each other's company, complimenting Mellette on her cooking. It came as a surprise to her, since cooking wasn't exactly her strongest suit. Many nights, at the beginning of her marriage, Landry would endure the meal, tell her it was good, and eat small portions, feigning a small appetite. What she hadn't known at the time had been that he'd eaten the small portions because that had been all he could endure. Then later he'd sneak into the kitchen and fix a peanut-butter-and-jelly sandwich.

They'd been married almost a year when she'd caught him with a peanut-butter sandwich in his hand. At first he'd tried sparing her feelings, telling her it was because he loved peanut butter and jelly, then he'd finally, after some persuasion, owned up to the lie and confessed that her cooking left a little to be desired.

So she'd tried even harder, and improved some. But tonight was such a triumph, having everybody praise her cooking and genuinely like it. Especially Justin.

"She'd make some man a fine wife," Charles Doucet said to Justin after Paul and Amos had gone home for the night and Mellette was showing Leonie all the changes she was making to the clinic. Justin and Charles were standing on the front porch, enjoying a rare cool breeze blowing through Big Swamp, both of them drinking tall iced tea accented with a little splash of sweet lemonade.

"Except she doesn't want that," Justin said, looking up at the sky visible through the thick bayou canopy, seeing patchy splotches of starless black.

"You sure? Because she sure seems to have the eye for you."

Justin chuckled. "I see where she gets her straightforwardness from."

"Her mama," Charles said, without missing a beat. "God never did put a more straightforward woman on the face of this earth than Zenobia Doucet. That's what got me hooked in the first place. I liked all that opinion in her. Made her different from all the other women I knew who went wishy-washy or giddy when asked their opinion.

That, and the fact that Zenobia's as fine looking a woman as I've ever seen. Just like Mellette."

"She *is* a fine-looking woman, sir," Justin said.

"You would be talking about my daughter, I'd hope," Charles responded, chuckling.

"I would be talking about all the Doucet women I've met so far." But especially about Mellette. Her dark skin, stunning eyes. The kind of woman who naturally flowed into a man's thoughts, even when he tried keeping her out.

"Well, all I can say is that I agree with you on that. And that it's going to take some kind of a special man to win the heart of my eldest daughter again. Landry is a tough act to follow, but I'm sure the right man can find his place with Mellette. He'll just have to work hard to prove himself. But if he's willing to do that, he'll discover that she's worth the extra effort."

"Tough order, though," Justin said, turning his face to the breeze. He used to love nights like this, where the weather went from an unbearable wet heat to cool and balmy. Of course, usually after the drastic change a storm rolled in.

Sometimes just a bad storm, sometimes something worse, like a hurricane. Tonight he didn't know what was coming, but his immediate concern was for the safety of Mellette, Charles and Leonie, because if they didn't get out of here soon, they wouldn't be getting out at all until the storm blew over.

"Look, not that I want to cut the evening short, because I don't. I've really enjoyed this. But if you want to get back before the storm hits, I think you'd better take Mellette and Leonie and start out now." He looked up again, hoping to see a star or two, but saw only the same somber blackness. And the breeze was getting even breezier. "Or maybe you should spend the night here."

Charles looked up, took his own appraisal. "And worry Zenobia to death? She's not fond of this place to begin with, but if she ever knew that I'd come out here and brought Leonie, she'd have my head."

"What's she going to do when Mellette starts bringing Leonie to work occasionally?"

"Well, right now she doesn't know about it,

and I'm keeping it that way for as long as I can. But once she finds out, she'll have *your* head, if you're still hanging around these parts. So, on that note, think I'll go round up my ladies and take them home."

"Sure you shouldn't stay here? It can get treacherous out there during a bad storm."

"Not as treacherous as my wife can get, so thank you kindly for the invitation, but I think it's best to, as they say, get while the getting's good. It's been a good evening, though, Justin. And I wish you success with what you want most." He gave Justin a knowing wink. "And I hope to hell you know what that is."

"I'm beginning to think I might," he said, with a sigh. "Yes, I'm beginning to think I might." On that note, he followed Charles back inside to say good-night to Mellette, a little bit nervous, especially now that he'd all but had her father's blessing and encouragement.

"She's in the kitchen, putting away the dishes," Leonie announced. "Grandpa went to help so we can go home fast."

"But you're not helping them?" Justin said, smiling at the girl. Her eyes shone with the same determination he saw in Mellette's eyes. Another strong woman in the making, he decided.

"Too short," she said, matter-of-factly.

"It's tough being short, isn't it?" he asked, heading on into the kitchen, holding out his hand to Leonie to take her with him. "But it won't last long. I promise. One of these days you're going to wake up and you won't be short anymore, and when you look at a picture of when you were short, you'll hardly even remember it because getting tall like your mommy happened so fast."

"Really?" Leonie said.

"Honest truth," Justin said, then bent and whispered to her. "I know, because I used to be short, too."

"Just like me?" Leonie asked.

"Once I was even shorter than you are. Then look what happened to me." He patted the top of his head. "I got this tall."

"Wow," the little girl said, totally taken by Justin and his story. "Will I be that tall, too?"

"Maybe not this tall. Or maybe taller. It'll be a big surprise."

"What surprise?" Mellette asked as Justin and Leonie stepped through the kitchen door, hand in hand.

"How tall I'll be," Leonie announced. "Did you know Justin used to be short like me?"

"Seems like you've got quite a way with children," Charles said, as he put away the bean pot.

"Look," Justin interrupted. "As much as I hate doing dishes, why don't you all let me finish this while you go home? I don't want you getting caught on a back road in the storm that's coming, and since your dad's insistent on getting home… the sooner the better."

"You'll be okay out here all alone?" Mellette asked sincerely, then realized that sounded a little patronizing. "Of course you will. What was I thinking?"

"You were thinking how you were concerned for a friend," Charles said, as he scooped Leonie up into his arms and headed for the front door. "A very good friend."

Both Justin and Mellette shot the man a reproachful look as he scooted outside, laughing.

"He wants me to be happy," Mellette explained, "and to him, happiness comes in the form of marriage."

"And seven daughters?"

"Probably. My dad is a very traditional man living in a family of eight very progressive-thinking women. It's not easy on him, but his heart is in the right place, even though he tends to get a little too concerned about our welfare and futures. Fact is, he would have had each of us married off years ago and producing all kinds of grandchildren for him to be fawning over. But we tend to take after our mother, who believes you can have it all—career, marriage, family—and a happily ever after that involves all of it."

"Well, he's very good in his role of father."

"Trying to marry me off?"

"Something like that."

Mellette blushed. "I'm sorry you got dragged into that, Justin. Daddy means well but, like I said, he's traditional. You know, as in a woman can't be happy or fulfilled without a man."

"And can she be?"

"Just the way a man can be happy and fulfilled without a woman. And on that note—" she headed for the door "—think I'd better catch up with them or my very traditional father will strand me out here for what he thinks is my own good."

Justin followed Mellette to the front porch and made a very big show of not getting too close to her so Charles would see there was no kiss involved. The strangest thing happened, though, just as she stepped off the front porch. He wanted to go after her. Wanted to pull her into his arms and kiss her like he'd never kissed another woman. "You shouldn't go out in this. I think it's going to be a bad one. I did ask your dad to stay overnight."

"We'll be fine," she said.

"You'd be more fine if you spent the night here."

"And I'll be better if I spend the night in my

own bed. Look, Justin. I appreciate your concern, but it's not a good idea to stay out here another night."

"Why?"

She shrugged. "Honestly, I don't know. Things are getting complicated. The absolutes I've been hanging on to aren't as absolute anymore, and it scares me. So I just want to…go home. That's all."

"What absolutes, Mellette?"

She shook her head. "I need time to think before I…before I say anything, or do anything."

"Would this be about me?"

"About you…about me. There was a time when I thought I couldn't move on, but now—" she shrugged "—it seems like I am, and I need to adjust to that before I say or do something that could affect my future or Leonie's or even yours."

"And the storm makes it convenient to run away."

She smiled sadly. "It does, doesn't it?"

"What if I convinced the three of you to stay,

and promise not to talk about anything meaningful?"

"Nice try," she said, reaching up to stroke his cheek. But before her hand reached him he took hold of it and kissed it.

"Nice try," he said back.

"Look, I've really got to go now. Daddy's a good driver. We'll be fine, like I told you."

"And like I told you, you'll be better spending the night here."

She shook her head stubbornly. "No," she said in finality. "We're going home."

"Call me when you get there?" he asked.

"If I remember. But I do have to get Leonie to bed first."

Damn, she was a stubborn woman. It was as sexy on her as it was frustrating. "How about you let me do the driving as I know the roads better?"

"I know the roads, too."

"Are you trying to run away from me?"

"Maybe a little bit. But we will be fine, and I'll call. I promise. As soon as I can get reception, I'll call and let you know we got home safely."

They could have argued it into the night, and she still wouldn't have backed down. Continuing the argument only kept them here longer, so he took a step backward, threw his hands in the air in surrender and frowned. "You win, but I don't like it."

"I always win, Doctor."

"But is it always for your own good?" Without warning, without provocation and without thought, he stepped forward, pulled Mellette into his arms and kissed her hard. It was short, because he truly hadn't seen it coming, but not so short that he didn't feel the effect of it shoot straight up through to his feet. Funny thing was, for a moment it seemed like she was kissing him back, just as hard, just as desperately. Lips pressed tight, breathing slightly heavy, all in the dim glow of the yellow lightbulb.

But from the kiss there was nowhere else to go but backward, so he did the gentlemanly thing and took that step back. He'd be damned, though, if he was going to apologize. He had nothing to be sorry about. Nothing at all. So he simply stood there and waited for Mellette to make the next move.

She raised her fingers to her lips and exclaimed, “Oh, my,” very, very quietly.

Oh, my, indeed. This was the second time she’d made him go weak at the knees. “Well, that’ll give your dad something to think about,” he responded. “Now I guess you’d better get going while you can.” Before the next kiss happened. And, hand raised to God, he wouldn’t let her go if he kissed her again. “Because if you don’t you really might have to spend the night here.”

On that note, she turned and hurried down to the car, crawled in, and then they were gone.

Justin watched until the car was no longer in sight, then returned to the kitchen to finish cleaning up, wishing he’d fought harder. But the harder he fought, the harder she countered him. Still, riding out the storm with her would have been nice. “So I’m getting myself hung up on someone who’s going to change my life in big ways,” he told Napoleon, who’d come around begging for his dinner. “Here’s the thing, are you content to be a Big Swamp cat, or do you think you could make it in Chicago? Because those are the choices." The thing was to have Mellette and to make her happy, there really was only one choice.

The cat answered with a coarse meow.

"To have her I have to stay. She'd hate being anywhere else but here. And I'd hate being anywhere where she wasn't," he continued as he pulled a can of tuna and egg scramble from the cupboard and opened it.

Napoleon's response was to arch his back and twine himself around Justin's ankles. "So that would be my answer, wouldn't it? Arch my back and entwine myself around Mellette's ankles forever. If she'll have me."

He dumped the cat food into a bowl and put it down on the floor. "See, you've got the right idea. Go where the food is. If I'm here, you come to me. If Mellette's here, you go to her. And if neither of us is here, you wait for Amos to come round and feed you. No games, no tricks, no wondering how it's going to turn out. You already know, and you go with it, no matter who's opening your can of tuna. Makes life easier doing the simple, obvious thing, doesn't it, boy?" He reached down and stroked the cat just as the first rumble of thunder hit the bayou.

It was loud and startled him, caused his breath to catch as it roiled on and on. He and his grandmother used to sit out of the porch and watch the storms roll in like this. That had been back when the lightning and thunder had scared him. "God's way of cleaning up the bayou," she used to say. "It stirs up the water, gets rid of the dead wood in the trees and gives everything a good washing."

Well, the good washing started even before Justin could get outside to watch it. Once he was there, he settled into the swing, watched the rain start to trickle down at first then eventually turn into torrential sheets. He missed his grandmother like crazy. And missed Mellette almost as much.

"You missed the turn," Mellette said to her dad as they crept past the road that would have taken them back to the main highway. The storm was pretty bad now, changed from a moderate shower to a torrential downpour in a matter of minutes, and while storms didn't normally bother her, she rarely spent them out in the middle of the bayou where their effects seemed larger, and louder, and more violent.

Justin had been right. They should have stayed there. But staying had meant confronting her feelings, and she wasn't sure she was ready to confront anything yet. Part of her wanted to, because her feelings for Justin were getting stronger. He was nothing like Landry, no similarities, no way to compare the two, which was good. Because Justin didn't deserve that and neither did Landry's memory. But that was all he was now. A memory who held a special place in her heart. Putting him in that rightful spot was so difficult. She had to do it, though, if she wanted to finally move on. It was time. Justin was showing her what her heart was telling her.

Mellette glanced over the seat at Leonie, who was thankfully slumped over in her car seat, sound asleep. "This one leads out to Grandmaison, and that's at the literal end of the road.

We need turn around and go back." Funny how well she knew this backcountry— it was almost like she'd grown up in it. Could she leave here, leave New Orleans and live in Chicago? There had been a time she would have said no. Now the line was blurred. There were no more definites; Justin was showing her how to move past them. So maybe Chicago could work. "There's a place just up ahead on the left where I think we can do it. It's a driveway, leads down to Amedee Mouton's property." She knew Amedee by the gout in his right big toe.

A tree branch came crashing down on the road in front of them, which brought the car to a stop. It was large, a main feeder from an oak tree, and it blocked the entire road, stopped their progress forward to Amedee's turnoff. While their recourse was to turn around and go back to the right road, there was no place to make that turn on a one-lane, dirt washout that artery was turning into. Plus the wind and rain were picking up, the visibility had decreased to only a few feet and the lightning was getting treacherous.

"Could we just back down the road?" Mellette

asked, turning around in her seat to get a better view out the rear window.

"We could, except I can't see the road well enough to negotiate it."

"Do you have a flashlight?" Mellette asked.

"In the glove box."

As much as she hated to suggest it, she said, "Then I'm going to get out and walk behind the car, and signal you where the road is."

"In this weather?"

"We don't have any other options, Dad. It's either keep moving or stay here until the storm passes and hope we can get out of here when it does." Much like the way she'd been living her life lately. Only in her life, she'd chosen to stay. "And I'd rather not get stranded on the road, which is what's going to happen if another tree branch comes down behind us. So how about we just get this done?"

"Can I help?" Leonie piped up from her car seat.

"No, sweetheart. Grandpa needs you to be very quiet so he can concentrate."

"You drive, I'll direct," Charles said. But Mellette was already out of the car and on her way down the road behind it. She'd never been out in rain like this. On a muddy, slippery road, with the wind gusting so hard against her she was afraid it would blow her right over. She was taking a risk that somehow seemed small compared to the one she was considering.

"Can you see my light?" she yelled, waving her flashlight in the air, in the direction of the car. "Dad, can you see it?"

If he responded, she didn't hear him because the wind was so noisy. In fact, all she could hear was her own voice blowing back at her and the low howling of wind whipping through the trees on all sides. It was eerie, being so close to the car yet so distant from it, and all she could do was trust that he followed her light and hope that whatever beasties lurked in the shadowy ditches to the side of the road were content to hunker down in the downpour, the way she wanted to.

It took Mellette nearly ten minutes to direct her dad down a stretch of road that should not have taken more than a minute to cover, and by the time they'd reached the intersection where he should have turned in the first place, she was exhausted, ready to climb back into the car and hope the rest of their trip out of the bayou was uneventful. But no such luck.

As Charles made the turn, and as Mellette was about to run to get in, a huge downdraft caught the car and spun it around, knocking it sideways into the ditch along the side of the road. In order to avoid being hit by the fishtailing car, Mellette took a leap sideways and landed flat in the mud, wrenching her shoulder and twisting her ankle. Nothing serious, but nothing she wished for in the middle of the storm, either.

"Dad!" she yelled, pushing herself out of the mud and trying unsuccessfully to rise above her knees. Between the rain, the wind, the mud and what was turning into a swollen ankle, all of that combined with no leverage from an unusable shoulder, she was pretty well stuck where she was, scared to death that either her dad or Leonie had been injured in the slide-off. "Can you hear me?" she yelled frantically, trying with everything she had in her to crawl or slither over to the vehicle. "Dad! Leonie!" Justin…

No answer, of course. And as she crawled along she worried about alligators in the ditch, and trying to get herself down the three-foot embankment. What if they were hurt? How could she help them? "Please, can you hear me?" She also worried about a flash flood coming through that could drown them. And the rain was getting worse. "Please, answer me. Or hit your brake lights or something to let me know you're okay."

No response again. So Mellette belly-crawled her way back down the road, too slow to make a difference but determined to get there no matter what it took, while feeling total despair, too worried to even think straight. Too worried to realize that anyone coming along that road stood a good chance of not seeing her there on the ground, belly to the mud, and hitting her before she could get out of the way. *What am I going to do?*

She shut her eyes for a moment, said a little prayer, hoped that when she opened her eyes this would be a nightmare, that none of this existed, that she was back at Eula's House, enjoying the evening with Justin, glowing in the praise of her cooking, showing her daughter what she was doing at work. But when she opened her eyes…

"Oh, my…"

The headlights bearing down on her didn't have her in their beam. She was there, directly in front of the vehicle coming at her, but there was no way she would be seen. And even though the car seemed to be traveling very slowly, that was just as deadly as fast. So she grabbed her flashlight, tried aiming it at the car to signal the driver, but the metal casing was slick and the light slid right out of her hands. A quick, chaotic patting of the muddy ground around her produced nothing. The flashlight was totally lost.

Frantically, Mellette tried scooting herself along in the mud faster, trying to get herself out of the path of the oncoming car. The slippery road made progress at a satisfactory speed nearly impossible in her position, as the road was already turning to small streams of rushing water, reducing her to the position of a fish fighting to swim upstream. So rather than trying to crawl any longer, Mellette lay down and simply rolled, hitting her wrenched shoulder repeatedly against the road, each bump and grind making her injury all the more painful. She just hoped she was fast enough, and the vehicle continued to be slow enough…

Praying there in the mud and rain that she had enough time to get out of the way, she worried about her daughter. "Leonie," she whispered as the vehicle slogged its way on past her, missing her by mere inches as her body slid off the road onto the grassy berm separating the road from the ditch on the right side.

Truth was, she wasn't sure she hadn't been hit. Her shoulder and ankle hurt so badly the pain radiated through her body like someone was prodding her everywhere with a hot poker, making her feel like everything in her body was aching, as well. Sympathetic reaction, she told herself as she stretched up, glad to see the lights from the vehicle coming to a stop near where her father had skidded off the road. *Thank God someone will help them,* she thought as she sank back down in the rain and the mud, closed her eyes and hoped to be found.

It wasn't that he had his grandmother's "extra sense," as she'd called it. But something wasn't right. He could feel it. He was restless. Needed to pace off the energy. Or go running. Anything. "Did she get like this when she knew something wasn't right?" he asked the big orange cat, who was sitting in the open window behind him, grooming himself, his back turned to the storm like it didn't matter that all hell was breaking loose in the bayou since his own tiny space in the universe was secured.

Justin had seen his grandmother suddenly "know" something on several occasions, and had never paid much attention to that peculiarity of hers. Thought it was crazy mumbo jumbo. But right now he wasn't so sure because his feelings were so strong they were about to drive him over the edge. So he bolted out of the porch swing and crashed through the door, then paced up the stairs then right back down for the next five minutes, every passing second making him feel even more pent up.

"They couldn't have made it all the way out of the bayou before this storm broke," he told Napoleon on one of these trips downstairs. He paced back upstairs, got to the top stairs and spun around, then ran back down. "So I'm going out. Back in a few minutes," he said to the totally uninterested cat.

Did it make any sense that he was going to drive all the way out to the highway? Probably not, but he didn't care. If a little drive in the worst storm he'd seen since he'd left Louisiana alleviated his anxiety, then it was all good. If it didn't, he'd take the highway on in to New Orleans, right up to their door, if that was what he had to do. What was he looking for? Nothing, he hoped. Absolutely nothing.

Hopping into his grandmother's old pickup truck, hoping it was up to the task, Justin made his way slowly along the road, glad with every passing few feet that aside from the storm and the occasional limb in the road, so far it was an uneventful drive. People didn't go out in weather like this, he thought to himself as he leaned forward to peer through a totally rained-over windshield with wipers so slow and worn they did little to disrupt the water on the glass. It was coming down in sideways sheets, hitting the truck so hard it sounded as if he was being attacked by falling rocks rather than the unremitting raindrops.

Traveling at no more than a few miles an hour, the trip was interminably long, and there was no visibility other than what the headlights picked up in their narrow beams. Even then those images were captured only mere inches in front of him, which slowed his five miles an hour to three when he thought of what he might miss if he traveled any faster.

What the hell had he been thinking, allowing Mellette and Charles to go out when bad weather was predicted, even though it had been their choice to try to get home? Back in Chicago there'd been bad storms, especially blizzards and windy thunderstorms coming off the lake, and somehow he'd forgotten that Chicago's very worst wasn't anywhere close to what Louisiana could bring on.

"They're going to be fine," he told himself as he literally inched his way along the dirt road, hoping his trip was uneventful and that they were already back in New Orleans, tucked away in that big, white mansion of theirs.

Still, he had to go on because…well, just because. If something happened to the three of them out on this road… Justin swallowed hard, blinked harder and tried to focus on the fraction of light he could see on the road ahead of him. It was there, then it was gone. A flash that could have been anything. Were his eyes playing tricks on him? Had he really seen something?

He slowed for a second, rolled down the truck window and looked out. Nothing. But that didn't mean anything, so he got out. Opened the door, stepped down onto the road that looked more like a shallow stream and took his flashlight, which unfortunately was only a medical penlight, and surveyed the area in front of him then off to the side of the road. And that was when he saw it—the shadowy outline of another vehicle sitting at an angle in the left ditch, which was approximately three feet below road level.

It was their car! That knowledge hit him like a punch to the gut, and he was away from his truck and crawling down into the ditch to assess the driver's side before he even realized what he was doing. Flashing his light in, he saw the air bag had deployed and was already deflating, with the white, powdery dust from the deployment still swirling around. He also saw Charles Doucet, who was caught somewhere between consciousness and unconsciousness, moving around, trying to extricate himself from his seat belt but not coherent enough to make the right moves to unlatch it.

"Charles!" Justin shouted, adjusting his angle to see Mellette. Only she wasn't in the front seat. So his eyes tracked back, saw a very frightened little girl strapped in her car seat, but still no Mellette. Had she been thrown clear, or was the white powder obscuring her? He didn't know, didn't have time to figure it out as he ran back up the ditch and climbed onto the passenger's side to get a better look. But still no Mellette. And the car wasn't open in any way, no windows had been shattered, so she hadn't just flown out on impact.

Stumped, he went back to the driver's side, fighting the rain that was turning the ditch into a stream, wondering where she was. Fearing the worst. He hated his fears, hated that he didn't know.

"We need to get the door open!" he shouted to Charles, who'd finally managed to beat down the entire air bag and was also free of his seat belt.

"Get Leonie first," he yelled.

"Are you injured?" Justin called back.

"Not badly. But I can't get back there to her."

"Where's Mellette?" he called, as he pulled on the driver's door, only to find it stuck shut.

"On the road. She got out to direct us. We slid off the road…haven't seen her."

And he hadn't seen her, either. Hadn't seen anyone. "Look, I need to go to my truck and get the crowbar." The one that had been under his grandmother's seat for as long as he could remember. *Emergencies, Justin. It's for emergencies.* "Thank you, Grandma Eula," he said to himself. "I'll be back in a minute."

The climb back up the ditch wall was easier said than done, as now the water was up to his knees and flowing hard and fast. Which meant he had to get Charles and Leonie out of there immediately, before the water level got so high… He'd heard stories of where a car trapped in a ditch got caught in a flash flood, and the water rose so high and so fast that it washed the car on down the stream into the lake.

Whether or not the stories were true, he really didn't know. But what he did know was that he had two people trapped in a dangerous situation and they needed to be out of there right away. So as he slipped and slid across the road, he shone his penlight back and forth, hoping to see Mellette. But he could see nothing. And he didn't have time to look. Damn it, he didn't have time!

Once he located the crowbar under the driver's seat he ran back to the car, slipped and fell headfirst into the wash, and realized that the water level was getting higher. He pulled himself up and made his way over to the car, where the water was now about halfway up the door.

Without a word to Charles, he stuck that crowbar in the door seam and put every bit of his weight into the effort of prying it open, and for once, thank God, luck was in his favor. The door opened with very little effort, and Charles practically fell into Justin's arms. "Get her out of the back," the older man gasped, as he tried to right himself.

In the backseat, little Leonie was crying and screaming for everything she was worth, kicking, flailing and clinging to her stuffed bear with ferocity. "Leonie," Justin said as he climbed over the seat into the back of the car. "Remember me?"

She stopped crying and looked at him. Then nodded.

"Good. Now, what I want you to do after I unbuckle your seat is to wrap your arms around my neck and hold on as tight as you can. Can you do that for me?"

"I want my mommy," she said, sniffling.

"I know you do, sweetheart, and I'm going to look for her once I get you out of here. So promise you'll hang on to me?"

She nodded. "My bear can't hang on."

"Then I'll have to put him in a safe place." Justin tucked the bear into his soaking shirt. "Now, grab hold..."

The struggle to get out of the car wasn't so bad, but the problem came in helping Charles up the ditch, and getting himself and Leonie back up the side, as well. It took several slip-and-slide attempts to get himself up to the road, but when he'd managed it he left the older man behind and got Leonie safely into his truck, then went back to help Charles make the climb out.

He lay flat on the ground and used every ounce of strength he had to pull Charles up and out of the ditch. The run-off was now threatening to suck him under, its wash was so turbulent. All the while he was scanning that ditch for Mellette, hoping she wasn't in it somewhere, because…because nobody could survive being submerged in that. "Do you have any idea where she is, sir?" Justin sputtered, once the man was seated in the truck cab, holding his granddaughter.

"She was on the road behind me."

"Behind?"

"I was backing up. Missed this turn-off, couldn't see the road well enough to negotiate it, so she took her flashlight and walked behind me, signaling the way. But I went into a skid, slid off… Don't know where she is, and the only reason she didn't come to help us… You've got to find her, son! You've got to find her."

"Are you okay for me to leave you?"

"Sore hip, that's all. No big deal."

Justin nodded, then shut the truck door and stood outside for a moment, trying to visualize the road and just where he'd seen that momentary flash of light. "Mellette?" he yelled, even though he knew his voice wouldn't carry over the wind. "Can you hear me? Do you still have your flashlight?"

There was no answer from her. That would have made things too simple—the whole rescue taking place without a hitch. Well, Mellette was his hitch, and the only way to proceed was to simply walk through the rain back the same way he'd been driving, an inch at a time. Looking for her. Hoping…praying she was okay. Praying even harder than she hadn't fallen into the same ditch the car was trapped in. The vehicle was now totally under water, bobbing up and down, getting ready to be carried off to wherever the ditch emptied. He couldn't bear to think that Mellette could be down there.

"Mellette," he screamed against the wind and the rain and the night, as he flashed his penlight along the berm and took it step by step.

She wanted to get up, but it was like there was a lead weight holding her down. As hard as she tried, she just couldn't get herself up to a sitting position. The pain had subsided some, reduced to more normal proportions, but her body was resistant, and she was so cold…so wet.

But she was awake, and if she fought to stay awake she'd be fine. She knew she'd be fine. But her dad and Leonie… She was so scared for them. Water could rush through these ditches with torrential force…. She should have listened to Justin and stayed there, instead of insisting they get back to town. But she'd been stubborn. Too stubborn. All because she didn't want to face the fact that she was falling in love with him and didn't feel guilty or disloyal.

For the first time since Landry had died, she realized she could move on and that it was starting to happen. She was starting over and it was scary and good and exciting and so many things she couldn't yet determine. But she wanted to start over now, because of Justin….

Heavy drowsiness slid over Mellette, trying to pull her into sleep. She fought it off, though. Fought it hard because back in E.R. she'd treated too many cases where unconsciousness had overtaken and killed people. She knew about exposure, knew about hypothermia…knew her body wanted to wind down and give up the battle.

"No!" she said. "I won't let it. For Leonie…have to fight." She had to stay awake until somebody found her. Until Justin found her.

"Justin," she murmured, picturing herself in his warm, dry arms. He'd come to get her. Would take her away, take her someplace safe. Protect her. "Justin…"

Five minutes of looking, then ten, then fifteen passed, but he wasn't giving up. She was out there, so close he could feel her. But he just couldn't… "What the…?" Off to the side of the road, on a grass berm, his light slid over a form. It didn't look human, wasn't moving…could have been mistaken for a rise in the weeds and fescue grass growing prolifically there. Or even an alligator crouching down, hoping to be ignored while he enjoyed the deluge.

Something compelled Justin to move to the side of the road, however, and there… "Mellette!" he shouted, kneeling down beside her.

"Justin, I knew you'd come. Knew you'd save

me," she gasped, throwing her arms up around his neck and clinging to him for dear life.

"Are you hurt?" he asked, as she buried her face to his chest. "Mellette?"

"I knew you'd find me. I was waiting… Knew you wouldn't let me die out here. Knew you would come looking for me…."

"Of course I would," he said, huddling over her to protect her. And just like that, her grip on him tightened and she kissed him. Kissed him hard, and with so much desperation…

A reaction to being safe, he told himself as he pushed himself off her and started to help her up. That was all it was. Just a reaction to being safe. A kiss anybody might give their rescuer out of gratitude, shock, fear.

Or maybe she'd hallucinated. Thought he was Landry.

It wasn't right, being jealous of a dead man. But he was. Which made him feel like hell.

CHAPTER NINE

WITH HER ARMS still snaked around his neck, and her head still pressed to his chest, there was nothing Justin could do to stop the feelings Mellette was causing to well up inside him.

"Justin," she said again.

He looked away, didn't even glance down at the woman in his arms for fear he'd yield to the temptation that wasn't rightfully his. "You're fine," he said stiffly as he fought his way back to the truck, trying to keep himself upright against the wind, trying to keep his mind just as straight against the sure knowledge that was soaking through his skin.

So what *did* you do when you were falling in love with someone who wasn't emotionally available? Because that was what he was doing. He was falling so hard he could almost see himself walking away from his Chicago life to come back here.

Just what was he doing? It was one hell of a question and it didn't have a good answer, even though it had been loitering around the edges of his mind for a little while now—loitering without being processed into full thought. The truth was, the answer was already there. Loving Mellette was all that mattered. "Wet, chilled, probably a little hypothermic, but you're okay," he reassured her.

"I knew you'd come," she sputtered again. "Was waiting for you to find me."

"Of course I would find you." And he'd never let her go.

"Leonie? Is she okay?"

"Leonie and your dad are just fine," he said as he approached the truck. "I got them out of the car and, other than being cold and wet, there's nothing wrong with them." Opening the driver's side door, he slid Mellette into the middle spot, next to her dad, who was holding Leonie on his lap, then climbed in after her. Her head immediately went to Justin's shoulder, not to her dad's, and she snuggled into *his* side, shivering, as he maneuvered a wide turn in the road, taking great care not to slide and end up in the ditch the way Charles's car had.

Of course, he was used to driving in these conditions. He'd started sneaking this very truck out for a drive when he'd been tall enough to both see over the steering wheel and reach the gas pedal. "This is going to be a bumpy ride," he said, meaning it more in the figurative sense than literally, because now, with her head resting on his shoulder, Mellette's hand rested on his thigh. And he was fighting the urge to enjoy it with everything he had. Wondering if maybe, just maybe, she wasn't, for once, thinking of Landry.

"Not bumpy," Mellette murmured, finally relaxing into a slump. "Nice." Then she drifted off to sleep.

By the time they were back at the house, she was practically sprawled over him, in a way that no father should have to see. Which was probably why Charles hopped out of the truck the instant the truck stopped, grabbed Leonie and ran into the house, leaving Justin there to deal with a very limp Mellette.

"Wake up," he said, trying to untwine himself from her. "Mellette, wake up. We need to get you inside."

"I'm awake," she said groggily.

He wasn't convinced, given the almost intimate nature of the way she'd draped herself over him. Awake, Mellette would have never done this. Would she? "Awake with both eyes open. I need to see both your eyes open and looking at me, Mellette. Both eyes…"

"I'll open them," she purred as her hand wound its way up his chest and stopped only after she'd stroked his cheek with her fingers.

"Stop it," Justin said, totally confused.

"Why?" she asked. "Don't you like it?"

"That's not the point," he said.

"The point is I can live in Chicago, if you want us there. That's what I thought about the whole time I was in that ditch. That I love you, and when you love someone, nothing else matters. I thought I might die out there and I didn't want to die without ever telling you that I love you."

"And I love you, too, Mellette."

"Which is why I can go to Chicago. Because nothing else matters."

"We'll talk about this when you're not so tired. Right now I'm going to carry you upstairs and put you to bed, so you can get all the rest you need."

"Thank you," she whispered, turning her face up to look at him as he lifted her into his arms and kicked the truck door closed. "For saving us. Thank you."

He loved the fact that she was so close that despite being covered with mud and grass and soaked to her skin she was still the most beautiful woman he'd ever seen…ever rescued. "Look, Mellette, we need to talk once you've rested. We both need to be clear headed."

"I am clear headed. If you want me, I'll go to Chicago."

"What if I want you here?"

"You'd stay?"

"I'd stay."

Her response was to sigh and press her head against his chest. Then she let him carry her up-stairs to a room where he sat her down gently on the bed.

She gasped from pain, which alarmed him. "Where do you hurt?"

"Shoulder, ankle. Nothing broken, I don't think."

"Maybe I should take a look..." Or maybe that was something he should get her dad to do, given all the confused feelings that were now springing up in him.

"I appreciate it, although I don't think there's much you can do to help me." She smiled. "I was a bit clumsy out there."

"You were out on the road in the dark in a bad storm, directing traffic on the road. It's a miracle you weren't killed."

"A miracle," she murmured.

"Look, let me get you a pair of scrubs, and once you've dried off and changed, I'll have a look at you. Okay?"

She nodded as she sank back against the pillows. “Okay,” she said as she fought to keep herself from drifting off.

“She’s on the verge of going to sleep,” Justin told Charles, who was scouting the kitchen for a good stiff drink of anything he could find. “Oh, and my grandmother kept it in the pantry out on the back porch. Called it her medicinal stash. Don’t recall ever seeing her drinking it, but she did keep it handy for her patients.”

“My wife keeps it locked up because one of my daughters had a problem. Not that Delphine would get herself into trouble again, because I don’t believe she would ever do that. But Zenobia doesn’t want her daughter tempted. In fact, it’s only recently that she would even allow alcohol of any sort back in the house.” He chuckled. “And I’m not sure but I think she measures it each and every time one of us has a drink, which for me isn’t too often since I’m diabetic.

“She’s a formidable woman.”

“You can say that again,” Charles said, disappearing round the corner to the pantry then reappearing with a bottle of whiskey. "So care to join me?"

"Actually, I need to take some dry clothes up to Mellette then have a look at her. I guess she hurt herself when she fell."

"And just how would you be looking at her, young man?" Charles asked.

"Like a doctor, sir."

"That's too bad. I really thought you had more in you than that." He poured himself a small amount of whiskey into a glass, then drank it down in a quick gulp.

"I do, but I'm not going to let it be a problem."

"Let it be a problem. That's what my daughter needs, and for you the reward will be worth the hard work. Back in the day, when I was trying to decide if I stood a shot at winning the attention of the fair Zenobia, I almost tripped myself up thinking about all the bad aspects. First, there was her status. She came from wealth, I didn't. And she always had this huge sense of rightness about her, one that could have scared me if I hadn't been so damn smitten. Of course, I never thought I had a chance with her. Even when she was in medical school you could tell she was destined for great things."

"Becoming an anesthesiologist is pretty great, too."

"It is. But with Zenobia…there was more there than I'd ever seen in any woman I'd ever met. And you know what? While I was still trying to convince myself to walk away, that I didn't stand a chance with her, she was the one who approached me, asked me out on our first date. And was I scared to go? Lord knows, I was shaking in my shoes."

"But you went and, as they say, lived happily ever after."

"Happily ever after," Charles said. "The thing is, I was on the verge of missing it all because all I saw were obstacles. And yes, my sweet Mellette has obstacles. But don't let that happen to you, son. Don't miss out because of them. Mellette may be like her mother in a lot of ways, but those are a joy to discover and an even greater joy to grow old with. So go get her settled in while I go and make sure Leonie's asleep. I've got her bedded down in one of the rooms upstairs, and unless you have other plans for me, I think I'll just give my wife a call if I can get through, then sleep there beside my granddaughter in the chair."

"Sorry I don't have better accommodation, but Mellette has been changing this place around so quickly…"

"And doing a fine job of it," Charles said with pride, as he tucked the bottle back into the pantry then headed back up the stairs.

Justin wasn't long after him, carrying a set of scrubs in his arms. "Mellette," he said, knocking quietly on the bedroom door. "Can I come in?"

Sure, it was a polite formality, but he needed to be polite with her. Besides, her dad was just next door. "Mellette?"

"Justin?" she said.

He pushed the door open, and the vision of Mellette Chaisson propped up against his pillows was almost more than he could bear. "Dry scrubs," he said. "Not much, but under the circumstances…" He sat them on the bed, then backed away.

"I might need some help," she said. "I'm not moving so well. My shoulder hurts. And my ankle is ridiculous."

"Let me get your dad…."

"I'm not having my dad help me dress. All I need you to do is steady me when I stand up and walk into the bathroom to wash myself off. And steady me when I do that, too. Oh, and you can keep your eyes closed if the sight of a naked woman bothers the good doctor."

"It doesn't bother me so much as I'm trying to be polite, as your father is right next door."

She laughed as she scooted to the edge of the bed. "Just kidding. I'll be fine on my own. Mind if I use the shower?"

Justin rushed across the room to help her stand, steadying her with his arm around her waist as he assisted her to the bathroom, where he did the gentlemanly thing and kept his eyes shut when she dropped her muddy clothes to the floor. But even with his eyes shut, his imagination went to town as he stood there and let her hold on to him, lean on him and anything else she wanted. "You know I'm just a poor mortal," he said when his head bowed down and his eyes opened to see all her clothes on the floor around her ankles.

She laughed. "A poor mortal who wouldn't take advantage of a woman in my condition. Now, could you turn on the shower for me and help me hobble in?"

Help her? Did she think he was made of stone? Especially when one look was so close that his hands were shaking. But in spite of the beast inside that wanted to look, or ogle, or even fondle, he completed all his tasks with closed eyes, holding his breath until she was safely in the walk-in shower, leaning against the wall, and he was safely back outside it, leaning against the bathroom sink. Sweating.

"I'll just be a minute," she said, as the water splashed off the sides of the shower.

"Take your time." He wasn't ready to help her back out and do it the gentlemanly way. Being a gentleman was taking everything he had.

"I'm really not that modest," she said. "Besides, you're a doctor."

"I really don't need to see you naked. Especially since if I did it wouldn't be the doctor in me doing the looking." And that was a huge understatement.

"I might not mind. But whatever the case, can you hand me the towel? I've stood on one leg as long as I can and I'm ready to get out."

He handed her the towel then the scrubs when she asked, and before long Mellette pushed back the shower curtain to reveal a very clean, very fresh version of her former muddy self. "You look better," he said, exhaling a sigh of relief now that she was fully dressed.

"A nice shower is a miracle unto itself," she said, hobbling out as he rushed up to steady her. "So let's talk about you staying here. Was that real or my imagination?"

"As real an offer as I can make. Back in Chicago all I have is…stuff. Nothing I love so much that I couldn't walk away from it. Here, I have something I love, but more than that, someone.

I'm in love. And that's the definition of *home,* isn't it? I want to come home, Mellette. To you, to the life I need to live. All of it."

"Are you sure?"

"Are *you* sure?" he asked.

"You know, you're pretty muddy. I think you need a shower." She dropped her towel to the floor. "Want somebody to scrub your back?"

Life was good here in Big Swamp. He had a new family, a new medical practice, and Eula's House was up and running and, surprisingly, busy. So much so they were already expanding. He worked there, alternating duty with Charles and several of Mellette's sisters and assorted friends. Mellette was the glue that kept it together, and with all the improvements made to the facility she was able to have Leonie at work with her every day now. That made for one happy nurse.

"It's what Eula wanted," Amos said as he and Justin sat on the porch swing, waiting for Mellette to see her last patient of the day. "She told me the first time she set eyes on Miss Mellette that she was the woman who would make you happy once and for all. I only wish she would have lived to see it happen."

Justin hadn't worked out all his guilt over his past, and maybe he never would. But it was amazing how much better he felt knowing that he was moving forward in the direction his grandmother would have wanted. That, and having Mellette's support made coming home to stay much easier.

"If that's what she wanted to happen, I'm sure she knew it would," Justin said, looking out to the fenced play yard where Leonie and several of her Big Swamp friends were playing ball together. There were so many kids here some days it was like they were running a day care. In fact, he and Mellette were thinking about adding that to the clinic's future agenda.

"So are the local folks treating you better out here now, boy?" Amos asked.

"A little. I have a few patients who ask to see me now and a couple who, when they end up with me, don't object. It's only been six months, so give it time." Time—something he never took for granted now, thanks to Mellette.

"He's being modest," Mellette said as she stepped outside and took her place on the swing next to Justin. "He has at least fifteen patients who like him, and probably that many more who tolerate him." She took hold of Justin's hand, then leaned over and kissed him on the cheek. "And one of his most faithful patients is Paul LeCompte."

Amos blinked. "You got Paul going to a real doctor on a regular basis? I don't believe it."

"I'm compromising," Justin admitted. "Giving him some of what he wants in return for him taking some of what I want him to. It works out."

"Look, we'd better round up Napoleon and Leonie and head back to New Orleans. Mother's expecting us for dinner, and we need some time to get ready."

Justin looked at Amos. "When my mother-in-law invites us, it's mandatory."

"Good Lord, man, you've surely been domesticated."

"That's what love will do to you, Amos. That's what love will do." With that, Justin pulled Mellette to her feet, grabbed the cat out of the clinic, and the two of them went to get Leonie. A core family of three with such a large family extending out from that. He was a lucky, lucky man.

"Do I have to wear a tie?" he whispered to Mellette as they headed to the boat.

"Tie. Shoes. Socks. Jacket." She kissed him then laughed. "Either that or a face-off with the Doucet family."

The thing was, he *had* faced everything. And he'd won the biggest prize of all.

"Oh, and about that last patient of the day…" Mellette said, placing Justin's hand on her flat belly. "It was me."

"As in…"

She nodded as the three of them walked along, hand in hand in hand. "As in."

Yes, he had definitely won the biggest prize of all. Somehow Justin knew Bonne-Maman Eula was up there, looking down and smiling.

* * * * *